VOICELESS

VOICELESS

CAROLINE WISSING

thistledown press

Thistledown Press Ltd.
118 - 20th Street West
Saskatoon, Saskatchewan, S7M 0W6
www.thistledownpress.com

Library and Archives Canada Cataloguing in Publication

Wissing, Caroline, 1968-
Voiceless / Caroline Wissing.

Issued also in an electronic format.
ISBN 978-1-897235-98-0

I. Title.

PS8645.I82V65 2012   jC813'.6   C2012-901132-0

Cover photograph: *Respect the Kid,* istock photo
Cover and book design by Jackie Forrie
Printed and bound in Canada

 Canada Council   Conseil des Arts
for the Arts   du Canada
 SASKATCHEWAN
ARTS BOARD
 Canadian   Patrimoine
Heritage   canadien

Thistledown Press gratefully acknowledges the financial assistance of the Canada Council for the Arts, the Saskatchewan Arts Board, and the Government of Canada through the Canada Book Fund for its publishing program.

ACKNOWLEDGEMENTS:

I am deeply grateful for the love and support of my family. My parents were the ones who thought: How about riding lessons? And to them I owe my life-long love and affection for all things horse-related. Thanks Mum and Dad. Jeff, Cameron and Jenna, without your humour and grace (and space) this novel would not have been possible. You are my everything.

I wish to thank my first readers: Bev Panasky, Gayle Chiykowski, Lucianne Poole, Melanie Curtis Raymond and Janet Di Giacomo. Your advice and support on this book were immeasurable.

Thank you to Thistledown Press for taking a chance on a first-time novelist, and to my attentive editor, Michael Kenyon, for being a stickler and making this story better than I thought possible.

Thanks to all my friends for their ongoing support.

I would also like to acknowledge the rich storytelling history of the North American indigenous peoples, from which I adapted Grandmother Spider's fire story.

For Jeff, Cameron, Jenna and Mum.
And in loving memory of my father.

Chapter 1

Graydon Fox arrived in a storm of dust.

Bobby Gervais's pickup truck stopped out front of the house, shimmering chrome in a haze of heat. Half the dust cloud settled into the dirt of the driveway, and half billowed through the heavy air.

My foster mother refused to tell us a thing. With a slight smile on her fleshy face and a tilt of her head, Mary Gervais knew every secret in a bucketful of secrets about the past of every new kid, but she would reveal nothing except a name.

With the news of an up-coming arrival, we kids — especially Tully, who couldn't wait for anything — begged and cajoled, pulling on Mary's sympathies and promising her everything we didn't have — the moon, the stars, a million dollars — for a shred of information.

I appreciated Mary's silence. I sure wouldn't want everyone knowing my story. It was mine alone to tell, or not to tell. I didn't really have to worry about telling anyone anything, though. I hadn't spoken a single word in a long time, which was mostly terrible but was also sometimes useful because it meant I'd never say anything I might regret later.

That summer afternoon I sat on a cane chair in the heat of the wooden porch with a sweaty glass of lemonade, both too sweet and too warm, on an up-turned plastic milk crate beside me. I jabbed at the peeling porch paint with the toe of my running shoe. The paint, dirty with boot tracks on top, and as white as new snow on the underside, came away from the old grey wood in one long strip.

I stayed on the porch and waited, poking at the paint with my toe and biting the skin at the base of my thumbnail. From the other side of the truck I heard Bobby's door squeak open and saw his feet drop to the ground. The dark shape inside the cab pushed the passenger door open and two thin white legs unfolded, followed by an equally thin body.

Curiosity pulled my hand up to shade my eyes against the glint of metal in the sun.

Graydon looked small for an older boy, maybe even shorter than me. It was hard to tell from where I sat. He moved with quick sureness when he wrenched the door closed with a sharp *thunk*.

Age was always the first thing I tried to guess, before the new kids blurted out every detail about themselves. I guessed fifteen, older than me by at least some months, for sure, despite his small size.

He went to the back of the truck and grabbed the handle of his suitcase before Bobby G could get a hand on it. He heaved it over the tailgate to the ground and carried it up to the porch steps in his right hand, leaning hard to one side against its weight, his other hand waving free.

When he entered the shadows of the porch overhang, I saw his face, nose wrinkled and lips drawn down toward his chin. He spotted me on my rickety wooden chair and said the first words I ever heard him speak.

"It stinks here," he said without stopping.

A thrill went through me as he passed by, and I felt the hundreds of little hairs on my forearms stand up despite the heat. His body let off a tight energy, an exciting kind of power, nuclear, that could suck you in and never let you go.

"Heya Ghost," Bobby G said with a nod. He smiled at me while he held open the screen door and Graydon Fox crossed the threshold of the house at Noble Spirit for the first time.

I turned away from the door, resisting the urge to follow Graydon and Bobby into the cool house. Trying to mask my eagerness, I got up and slouched down the front steps one by one. But the moment my left toe hit the gravel, I was off. I ran slantways, through Mary G's flowerbeds, and across the lawn, over the low hedge like a hurdler and straight up to the pasture fence.

The sweet scent of manure rode the heat and I sweated, leaning against the fence rail, catching up on the breath I'd left behind.

I watched as Jett, a small horse, black with white socks, ripped a hunk out of a pile of hay that lay spread across the sick-looking grass, yellowed with summer drought. Jett liked to throw it in the air, shaking out the stray pieces, before he pulled it into his mouth with soft lips. Comforted by him, his big shaggy body and slow breath only a few feet from me, I sighed and climbed up onto the top of the fence. I wrapped my summer-bare legs around the rail and leaned my back against the fence post.

I planned still to see Jett when I went off to live with Mama. She and I would settle close by, like in Ottawa or Kingston — because Mama liked the city life — and I would come back to Noble Spirit and visit Jett whenever I wanted.

Old Jett lumbered toward me, his head swaying from side to side with the effort. He nuzzled my fingers, his breath moist in my palm. I reached into my pocket and pulled out a rubbery carrot. I bent it double but it refused to break, so I let him bite it from my grasp in chunks, bit by bit.

I got down from the fence and rubbed around his eyes. He heaved a big sigh and closed his eyelids in bliss. I imagined his uncomplicated horse mind, blank and smooth as an egg.

Understanding between us didn't need any words. And everything else, from his stance to the position of his ears, told me what I needed to know. One ear cocked and the other indifferently swiveled to one side, said, "Oh, your pockets are empty today. What a shame." His feet wide apart and head hanging low said, "My back is killing me."

He seemed to sense when I was unhappy and knew the right moment to stick his nose down the front of my shirt. Sometimes we only wanted to hang out and be together, and I would hum a low tune into the softness of his muzzle. Spending time with Jett was my escape, like a dream world.

In the real world, having no voice was like being stuck in a nightmare, that nightmare where danger looms but screaming is impossible, where you're suddenly falling or choking, or you have feet made out of chunks of lead.

While I stood and stroked Jett's dark velvet ear, I ached to thieve a million answers about Graydon Fox out of the hot air — where he was from, why he was here, what had happened to him.

⋐⋑⋐⋑⋐⋑

Granny used to say that as a little kid I was a real chatterbox. She couldn't shut me up, and I asked so many questions, endlessly wanting to know about how the world worked, that she started refusing to answer in the hope I'd stop. There was no mystery I didn't want her to solve for me: rainbows, blue sky, God and death. These days my old chatterbox ways seemed pretty ironic.

Granny, who had kept me safe in the way a farmer might put blinders on his carthorse — so he doesn't get spooked and hurt himself — was a National Geographic addict. One of those people with stacks of yellow-spined magazines on every spare shelf. Searching for some peace and quiet, she sent me to the bookshelf whenever she got fed up with my endless jabbering. It was between those golden covers I saw my first full-length naked man.

In one of those National Geographics I also once saw a photograph of an iceberg. Why did I remember it? Probably because of its beauty, rising majestic from the water, cool blue shadows hiding in the nooks and crannies of its surface. But the photo on the next page really got to me, the photo of the iceberg's awesome lie. I always wondered how the photographer got that shot; it showed that the iceberg was only peeking above the surface. The rest of that block of ice hid under the water, like a massive secret. I was stunned and amazed at that crazy iceberg, able to successfully hide so much of itself.

Chapter 2

Ghost was my nickname. I had been called Ghost for so long I would've forgotten my real name, except I could still hear it in my memory, Mama's voice calling out from the time before: *Annabel.*

Mama. After I stopped living with my mother, her intrusions into my life were sporadic, but treasured. Infrequent treasures, like Granny's strong hand rare upon my shoulder, like a spring robin on the windowsill in the early morning. But Mama would come for me in the fall, so I only had to wait out the summer at the farm. For a while longer, I could be Ghost instead of Annabel.

I wished I weren't a girl at all. Girls could be hurt in worse and different ways than boys, and mine was such a girlish name. It sounded like a cow's name. I remembered Granny taking me to the Experimental Farm the summer I turned twelve, the thick stench of the cow barn, bits of hay dust dancing in sunbeams that slashed through the open barn door. All the cows had names like mine, printed on plaques of wood suspended on chains above their massive heads: Cassandra, Angelina, Noella. Why did a cow need a name, anyhow?

☙❧☙

That evening at the farm, supper descended into its usual fight over table space and food, a civil war of endless bickering, tinkling spoons and scraping knives. Tully screeched that Big Jerome had taken the last slice of sourdough bread. Charlene proclaimed social outrage that Big Jerome had stuffed the entire slice in his mouth at once and begun whistling *O Canada*, wet crumbs flying onto Char's half-full plate.

Only Graydon and I sat in observing silence. I looked at him when his eyes were elsewhere, and looked away when his gaze wandered toward me.

I was about to put my hands over my ears, sure my head would pop with the noise, when Mary G got to her feet, and the din dwindled to silence.

"All right, let's get busy. Char, sweetie, you clear the plates to the kitchen tonight. Jerome, help Charlene. Ghost, it's your night to wash up while Mr. Tully dries."

Mary reached out to Tully, who sat to her right, and patted the top of his head once. He pulled his shoulders to his ears and rolled his eyes as if embarrassed, but I knew he loved even a moment of Mary's attention.

"What about him?" asked Big Jerome, a brown-sausage finger levelled in the direction of Graydon.

"It's Mr. Fox's first night in our home. He's coming into the living room with me and Bobby to tell us as much of his story as he's willing to tell. He'll get his chores come tomorrow morning."

His arms resolutely crossed, Graydon pulled his body out of the kitchen chair, pushed past Mary's bulk and disappeared through the living room door. Bobby G stood. He took Mary's hand and led her through Graydon Fox's wake and into the living room.

While I watched them go, I thought of my own first meeting with Mary and Bobby G. I could still hear the clock ticking away the seconds of silence. Mary had rescued me with a hug and, smothered in the flesh of her bosom, spicy-sweet like lavender and talc, I began to cry. Misunderstanding, they tried to soothe me, to tell me everything would be all right. I hadn't been hugged like that in a long time, and crying was all I could manage to do.

The click of the closing door latch signalled to the rest of us like the pop of a starter's pistol. Whipped into a sudden frenzy, we gathered in a group at the kitchen table, like flies on a blob of honey.

"Holy crap. I wonder what's up with that guy?" Char scraped the bone of a pork chop from one plate to another.

"What the hell do you mean?" asked Jerome. "He looks like an ordinary guy to me."

"He ain't ordinary, I can tell you that much."

"What makes you say he isn't?" asked Tully.

"I seen guys like him before," Char pointed her sharp chin at the closed door. "He's trouble."

"You stupid anorexic snot-nosed cow," said Jerome, pausing to allow his string of insults to properly sink in. "You're so full of crap."

"Shut up, Jerome, you sack of monkey worms."

"Monkey worms? You suck. What does that even mean?"

Char lowered her head and glanced at each of us and then at the back of the living room door. We huddled closer, responding to her drama. "I think we should be careful, that's all."

We disbanded and the ominous spell of Char's words hung over us for a moment. Jerome and Char moved from table to kitchen counter and back again in a silence that wasn't like them at all.

Then Char sneezed and Jerome shouted, "Screw you," which was his current standard sneeze response, and in an instant everything fell back into place.

"Shut up, asshole."

"Why don't you go puke up a lung?"

"Why don't you go eat moose shit?"

Jerome and Char weren't finished insulting one another yet but I turned and filled the sink with soapy water. Tully got a clean dishrag from the bottom drawer. He climbed onto the wooden step stool and waited for me to wash the first dish. He smiled and I smiled. He leaned in. I stooped. "I agree with Char," he said. "I don't get a good vibe from this new guy."

I handed him a dish still steaming from the hot rinse.

"Do you know what our brilliant resident genius did last summer?" Jerome indicated Char as if she were an appliance on a game show.

We waited for the insult that we knew was coming.

"She shaved her *arms*."

"I thought you were supposed to," Char said, in a feeble defense. "You know, like you're supposed to shave your legs."

"I rest my case." Jerome bent in an elaborate bow.

"You're a jerk."

We finished the kitchen chores, almost expecting their completion to be the bell that ended Graydon's interview, but he still didn't come out of the living room. I wandered outside to sit on the porch and listen to the night.

Creatures made the night alive. During the day, noise got all gummed up because of sunlight and distractions. But at night, the world squirmed with living sound. A cicada buzzed in the humid air, bullfrogs bloated out their throaty sex songs, crickets chirruped in the throes of a wild party.

I got up and walked a slow circle in the front yard. I smelled the dewy grass and felt it tickle up the sides of my feet. There was hope in a blade of grass, in the vulnerable greenness of its tiny struggle. I remembered how I cried one day in early spring, my first spring at Mary's, when I got down on my belly, right up close, and watched one pale and slender blade nodding in the warm wind. There it grew, after months of winter so cold and violent that on some days you could hardly breathe, and snow so heavy the bushes came out bent and warped. When I'd got up from the ground, my jacket wet with dark mud, I saw other single pieces of grass here and there. I could almost feel them growing and multiplying into a lawn around my feet, into a whole field. A blade of grass is never alone for long.

From that first moment on, I felt part of this natural world, part of the trees, the dirt, the soft breeze. There was hope among growing things, where I forgot about Mama, Granny and all my silent fears. I only had to go in the fields alone to feel as if I were part of something bigger than myself. I could be a hardy blade of grass, growing greener and stronger with each passing day.

I vowed to have a place like this of my own one day. I didn't need acres and acres. Just a plot of land where things might breathe and grow. I barely dared hope to take Jett to such a place. Mary would let me have him if I asked, one less horse mouth for her to feed. I pictured Mama coming for a visit, and Mary.

It would happen because I would make it happen, no matter what occurred between now and then. I deserved a small patch of happiness. I really believed I did.

I sat on the bottom porch step and listened to the horses in the back pasture shifting their bulk and snuffling into the darkness. I longed to visit Jett and feel the heat from his body meet the heat of mine, but Mary and Bobby G didn't allow us to go to the pasture in the dark.

"Let 'em enjoy the peace of darkness like they never did where they came from," Mary always said about the horses. She would wave a beefy hand vaguely in the direction of the pasture, her wristwatch looking small, nestled in the fat at the crease between hand and forearm.

Only the week before, Tully, Big Jerome and I lay in the straw in the loft of the big hay barn and Tully joked that when Mary and Bobby stood next to each other, they looked like a bowling ball beside a pin. I stole a guilty smile. Tully hadn't meant any meanness by it, and the image was true blue. Mary was enormous and Bobby the toothpick opposite. They looked as mismatched as a married couple could look but they got along, most times, as if they shared a soul.

Big Jerome had laughed loudest at the bowling joke. He was pure Ojibwa Indian with a face like a full moon and a mouth stuffed with ready insults. He told us he'd been raised partly by a grandmother with a PhD in verbal abuse and he was determined to follow in her moccasins. If he got in what he thought was a good shot at somebody, he'd say, "Grandma'd be proud of that one."

By the time I went back into the house from the porch, the kitchen was deserted, dark and quiet. The door to the living room stood open. I peered around the jamb to see Mary and Bobby in their usual places on the couch, their faces bluish-grey with the flickering of the television screen. Mary looked up at me.

"The new boy's gone straight to bed. You can join me and Bobby, or you can head up to bed yourself."

I watched television sometimes, but didn't care much for it. Life wasn't like that, and it gave me a headache, so I went on upstairs to my room.

Mary once said that the original farmhouse was only the main floor, with the big kitchen and living room, and half the upstairs, which would have been only three rooms: two bedrooms and a bathroom.

Now the rooms of the house sprawled like spokes on a broken wheel, all haphazard and random. There were two extra bedrooms stuck onto the main floor, one off the living room, the other off the kitchen. And two rooms had been added on the second floor, over the garage. All the additional rooms, mine included, were sweltering in the humid weeks of summer and frigid in the depths of winter. Fans and space heaters had to make the rounds because there were too few of both.

At least each of us kids had our own room, which gave us more privacy than some of us came from. Only Tully, who never wanted to sleep alone, was bothered by it. By midnight every night he'd make his way into someone else's bed. If it got overcrowded with too many kids, Tully would gladly give up his room and bunk more permanently with Jerome. Strictly speaking, as a boy, he wasn't supposed to sleep with any of the girls, but we all kept quiet so Mary and Bobby wouldn't find out.

In my sauna of a room, the humid night squeezed beads of sweat onto my skin. The moist breeze from the open window didn't make it any cooler; it only made it damper. I put on a pair of boy's boxers and a white cotton tank top, and slid under a single sheet, kicking the blanket off the end of the bed and onto the floor.

I lay in the dark with my hands clasped behind my head, the musky smell of my armpits wafting in and out like a comfort.

I heard the floorboards groan outside my bedroom. The door creaked slowly open and the grainy outline of a very small person appeared, backlit by the nightlights that lined the hallway.

"Ghost?" whispered Tully. "Can I come in?"

I pulled one sweaty hand out from behind my head and flipped the sheet back.

"Thanks."

He leapt across the room, because he was afraid of monsters under the bed, and landed beside me.

Tully was the smallest almost-grown person I had ever seen. Granted, he wasn't an adult yet but, at sixteen, he was still a hair under four feet tall.

"I'd like you to measure me tomorrow. I think I've grown a little since last time."

I nodded, but didn't hold out much hope. He'd been three feet eleven inches for the past six months. Using a pocket knife we gouged height markers into the wooden frame of his closet door to keep track.

He once told me he planned to kill himself if he didn't get over the four-foot mark by his eighteenth birthday. I didn't believe him, though. He talked big, about jerks he planned to beat up if he got the chance, things he'd say to people if they were standing right in front of him. His talk was bigger than he was, that was for sure.

Tully was born with dwarfism, so his parents had thrown him away. They hadn't even taken him home from the hospital, not for one day. He'd been in foster care all his life and had told me most of his stories. Some of the foster families were nice, like Mary and Bobby G, and some were horrific. They were the reason he didn't sleep alone and was afraid of monsters under the bed at the ripe age of sixteen.

I looked at his profile in the grey light, his big, lumpy forehead and long chin. The stubby fingers of one hand lay spread over the top of the sheet. And then he kicked himself over onto his left side, facing away from me.

"Good night, Ghost," he said.

I turned over too, facing his back, his soft hair making dark swirls in the strip of light that shone through the crack under the door. Sometimes, when I looked at Tully, I saw myself. That's how close we were. My isolated body wanted to pull him to me, feel his heart pulse and lungs rise and fall, but my thoughts kept me distant.

If Tully pushed me away, I'd have one less thing to hope for.

◦-◦-◦

The next morning at breakfast, Graydon's sour look was gone and pure charm had slipped into its place.

"Let me clear the table," he said, and clattered the dishes into a pile on the counter.

"Charlene, it's your day to feed the horses," said Mary.

"It can't be. I just did it."

"Yes, you did, last week. Now it's your turn again."

Char rolled her eyes and stood, shoulders squared, thumbs hitched to the pockets of her tight jeans.

Mary sighed. "Please do as I ask, honey. Bobby and Jerome have already gone out to fix the back fence and won't be home until lunchtime. Those horses need their breakfast."

A sullen look pinched around her pretty eyes.

"All right, I'll do it."

"I'll help you." Graydon sprang to the front door and held it open for Char.

She took a hesitant step toward the door, swung her hair over her shoulder and stomped out. He followed her without looking back.

I stayed in the kitchen to help Mary wash up the dishes and sweep the kitchen floor. Afterward, Mary and I got the bowl of sourdough starter down from the top of the cupboards where it sat bubbling and fermenting. With the cloth pulled off the bowl, a good, yeasty smell filled the kitchen. I added a cup of warm water and stirred in a cup of whole rye flour to get the dough ready for baking by suppertime.

My chores done and the morning half over, I filled my pockets with carrots and small apples from the fridge and skipped out into the warming day. From behind me, I heard the screen door squeak open.

"Ghost, girl," Mary called, "don't feed those horses too many sweets, now. You'll rot their teeth clean out of their heads."

Without turning around, I waved once in acknowledgement. Mary cared about those horses as much as if she'd given birth to them herself. Mother Mary, mare, dam to us all who were rescued into her love.

I moved into a run, an easy lope, a canter that pretended four hooves tearing through soft earth. The wind, still tinged with slight morning coolness, fingered the short hair back from my forehead. I was free and alone, no one to judge or disapprove.

Rounding the fence, I went through the gate to the pasture, careful to latch it behind me, and walked to where the group of horses munched their breakfast of grain out of plastic buckets and rubber pans.

I pressed my cheek into the soft spot, warm and dusty, between Jett's jaw and the curve of his neck. He ate bits of apple from my palm and his working jaw bumped against my temple while he chewed.

Graydon's face appeared suddenly from the other side of Jett's head. Startled, I jumped and spooked Jett, who pulled his head out from between us and trotted to a safe distance, eyeing us both with annoyance and some suspicion.

"You like that horse, eh," Graydon said.

I shoved my hands into the shallow pockets of my shorts and looked at the bare and dusty ground.

"That's cool. I like horses too," he said.

My shoe scuffed a dark mark into the dirt.

"Can you help me?" He bobbed and ducked to try and catch my eye. "I told Char I'd fill the water trough for her, but I can't find the buckets."

Grateful to have a purpose, I looked him straight in the face and nodded once. I turned toward the stable and heard him fall into step behind me. The buckets hung on a peg in the barn, beside the feed bins. With one foot on a plank that jutted from the wall, I hoisted myself up and grabbed the nearest bucket off the peg. When I turned to hand it to him, his face was inches from my cheek.

"Thanks, Ghost."

His hand brushed mine as he grasped the handle of the bucket. I felt tall and foolish and let go of the handle before he had a good grip. The metal bucket clanged to the floor between us.

"I'll get it," and he reached down for the bucket without looking away from my gaze.

I felt held in place by his light-grey eyes, which were as see-through as two crystal marbles.

Chapter 3

I was standing outside in the paddock, pulling a comb through Jett's coarse mane, when I saw them.

It looked like a single deformed figure striding up the hill in the distance, a hunchbacked girl with long legs and hair like golden streamers. I knew this form, silhouetted by a halo of sun, was not one person, but two. Char stepped, sturdy and strong, over the lichen-covered rocks, through stands of goldenrod and long grass. Tully clung to her back, his arms around her neck, his tiny feet thumping against her buttocks. I knew they stole away from the farm almost every summer day, to the Reading Rock.

I kissed Jett and took time to rinse the comb and put it back into the grooming bucket. I went off after them, not worrying that I wouldn't find them. I knew exactly where Char had headed.

She turned sixteen this past spring and acted like she might walk away from Noble Spirit at any minute. She arrived a year ago, soon after me, as wild as some of the abused horses, and equally angry.

"I come from The Streets," she announced, almost proudly, to me and Tully one winter morning, while we worked our farm chores together. Tully stopped scooping grain and his eyes grew wide with fear of The Streets.

"When they beat you at home and beat you on The Streets," she said, "I pick The Streets every time. Least you don't expect anything else Out There."

Char had been one of the guinea pigs of a pilot project to get young prostitutes off Ottawa's seedy corners. Police rounded them up and offered them a choice: juvenile hall or foster care.

"Both of them options was a risk, that's for sure," she said. "But I done juvie before and didn't like it much. Thought I'd go for this one."

The first time I followed Char and Tully had been early last summer. Now I pushed through the overgrown meadow that had been a cornfield many years ago when a farming family owned the land. It had fallen fallow and now waved with wildflowers and hummed with throngs of busy insects. I loved it because of the birdsong on the breeze and the drifting scent of distant horses.

Human voices pushed the gentle buzz of nature out of my head. I edged closer to the source until I could make out Tully's voice, sweet and high, like raindrops in a puddle. He spoke on and on, his voice rising and falling in its rhythm. I lost myself in the stand of trees and dense bushes that grew along the fence line.

I inched forward. Tully was leaning against the smoothest side of the rock, his red baseball hat pulled down over his dark curls. It was such a perfect fit — Tully's back into the curve of the rock — that the boy and the rock seemed made for each other. Char lay across the grass, her head at Tully's feet, with a sprig of dry wild grass sticking out of her mouth.

Unusual, perfect contentment.

Tully held the book in his lap and tough-as-nails Charlene lay in the grass listening to him reading.

The first time I saw this tableau, I tutted to myself and shook my head. I almost gave myself away while they lounged beside their sun-soaked rock, but decided to leave them to their private moment, and all their private moments from then on. I didn't want Char and Tully to know I sometimes followed them out to the Reading Rock and listened.

I settled onto a rock of my own, cool from the shadows against the back of my bare thighs. I watched Char turn onto her stomach and pull a nail file out of her back pocket. She bit a piece of nail off her index finger and went to work on it with the file. Tully read on.

This situation had puzzled me at first because Char always acted like books would give her a fatal disease if she touched them. During the school year she didn't do homework in the evenings because she claimed she finished it in free periods. But I knew she spent free periods smoking behind the portables outside the shop wing door. She didn't even carry a backpack to school, just a little purse for her makeup and cigarettes, and a bunch of fruit for lunch stuffed into a crumpled brown paper bag.

One time, when we were all in the living room watching a TV commercial with a funny caption and Char's laugh came too late, I thought I'd figured out the reason for Char's book aversion. No one had ever bothered to teach her to read. I considered confronting her with this fact by offering to teach her myself. I fantasized about being her saviour and about how grateful she'd be. But the reality was she'd be so ashamed I'd get a solid Char smack-down for my effort. Plus, how do you teach stuff to someone when you don't have a voice? So I never did anything about it.

Out at the Reading Rock on summer days, along with Char, I'd heard Tully read *Treasure Island, Watership Down* and *The Lord of the Rings*. I'd watched her through my own tears as she wept for Black Beauty. Something familiar stirred in my heart for sour Miss Mary in *The Secret Garden*, the unloved orphan, abandoned to solitude on the misty moors: *Mary, Mary, quite contrary*. Granny used to recite that rhyme to me when confronted with my own contrariness.

Now Tully was reading *The Hobbit*. He had only just begun and dwarf after dwarf was showing up at Bilbo's door, testing his hospitality, baffling him and depleting his stores of precious nibbles. When Bilbo opened his hobbit-hole door to yet another dwarf, Char let out a shriek of laughter. And Tully paused, smiling.

"Holy crap! Another damn dwarf? What the hell are they all doing there?"

"We dwarves have mysterious ways," Tully said.

She hesitated, as if she were uncertain whether she might have offended him. And then he laughed and she laughed, and I had to bite my tongue not to laugh right along with them.

Char was always impatient with the stories. She wanted to know everything all at once. Tully never told her to shut up, but never revealed a book's secret until the story was ready to give it up. He just kept on reading, hypnotic and mesmerizing.

I had read all the books before, but a tone in Tully's voice made the stories more real and more beautiful. He loved those old stories, and it showed. Other kids our age were probably sneaking peeks at online porn, dirty magazines, or something else to satisfy lustful teenage urges.

To outsiders, we might have seemed stunted, childish for our age, but we were simply happy for this sudden freedom to be ourselves. No one knew how long it might last. I believed we just wanted to crawl into the children we'd never had the chance to be.

⟡⟡⟡

I thought a lot about that moment when Graydon bent to pick up the bucket I had dropped, the electric zing of his hand on mine.

In the kitchen that second afternoon I overheard Bobby say to Mary, "That boy's a strong and able worker. As long as he can keep his mind to it, he'll be a help."

"I hope so."

A skeptical undertone to Mary's hope made me wonder what Graydon had said to them the night before. I waited for more information, but neither Bobby nor Mary appeared ready to reveal Graydon's secrets. I slid up beside Mary, hoping she would give me a chore to do that would keep me near her for a little longer. She turned right into me, almost losing her balance.

"Jesus, Ghost. You gotta learn to make some noise or something. Your creeping self is gonna scare me to death one of these days." She gave my shoulders a small squeeze as she passed by.

Mary gave me the nickname on my second day at Noble Spirit. She had stood at the same kitchen counter while I watched her strong hands, reassured by the sway of her large bottom. I wanted only to be near her, and Mary hadn't heard me come up. When she turned, she knocked me right on my butt. She helped me to my feet, apologized and said I was as silent as a ghost.

She'd sat me in a chair at the kitchen table, pushed the hair off my forehead with a finger. "Honey, some people who've seen things like you've seen want to change things about themselves when they're finally safe. How about I call you Ghost? Would

29

you like it if I did?" I'd nodded, leaving Annabel gratefully behind.

While Mary and I prepared supper, I wanted her to tell me Graydon's story, even though I knew she wouldn't. At the kitchen counter, she rolled out dough for a peach pie. I sat at the table with a colander of freshly washed peas, shelling them into a stainless steel pot. I ran my thumb down the back of the open pod and each pea, fat and round, jumped into the bottom of the pot, *plink, plink.*

"Did I ever tell you how Jett came to us?"

I shook my head, even though I'd heard it before, because I wanted to hear her tell it. I didn't know whether Mary believed the shake of my head or if she wanted to tell it again.

"Six years ago I'd never ridden a horse in my life and Bobby and me had just moved out here to the farm. There was all this space with no life in it. I was a lot thinner in those earlier days, so I said to Bobby one evening, 'I want to get a horse.' Bobby looked at me like I'd just said I wanted to chop off my own arm and feed it to the crows."

I smiled while I popped open another fat peapod.

"I didn't know anything about horses. But I was determined to find one and learn to ride it. I went here, there and everywhere and couldn't find the right one. Dang it, I didn't even know what I was looking for; I was so green. So this one day I saw an ad in the paper for a horse. Everything about it sounded right, so I called the lady and made an appointment. I pulled up to a farm about an hour south of Smiths Falls and there in the paddock was the sorriest looking horse you ever seen. I didn't even know how sorry looking he was cuz I didn't know anything about horses. He stood there with his nose right near the ground, not moving. The lady said he'd be perfect for me to learn to ride. 'He's quiet,' she said.

"I paid for him and brought him home here, so excited to finally have my own horse. I called up my friend Tammy and when she first caught sight of our Jett she almost died on the spot. 'You need a vet to come out and look at that horse, Mary,' she said to me."

Mary sprinkled sugar over the slices of peach in the pie. I shelled the peas slowly so Mary wouldn't stop the story and send me back outside to get up an appetite for supper.

"The vet just about popped his clogs when he saw our Jett. 'His teeth are bad, his feet are bad, he's got the worms and he's too skinny,' he said to me. But Dr. Frost, he fixed him up fine. Gave Jett medicine for the worms, cream for his hooves and told me what and how often to feed him to fatten him up. Yessir, Jett came along good after that.

"Except he hated me. Least that's what I thought. He wouldn't have anything to do with me, if I didn't have a treat for him in my pocket. One sniff and he'd walk away, ignoring me like I was nothing more to him than a fencepost. He'd walk right over me if I didn't get out of his way.

"Bobby, Tammy, Dr. Frost and everybody else said I ought to forget about keeping him. Sell him and buy a horse that would let me ride him, or at least let me near him.

"Then this one day I decided to stop getting out of his way. I squared my shoulders and stood my ground, and if it didn't beat all, that Jett went around *me* for a change. Things were different for us after that. We got respect for each other, him and me."

She leaned toward me. "Until I tried to ride the little bugger. What I was thinking, I'll never know. I stuck a borrowed saddle and bridle on him one day, swung myself up on his back, and he went wild. I could see white slivers of moon in his eyes while I sat helpless on top of him. He wheeled, bucked, did most everything to get me off him. And when I did slide to the ground, I was as shook up as if I'd lived through a car wreck.

"I don't know what those people before me must have done to him, but he was ornery as all get-out. It took another some few weeks, but we got the respect back between us.

"I never tried riding any horse again, not once. But it broke my heart to think of all those horses out there that were like Jett, all beat down with no life left in 'em. So I vowed that if I ever came across another horse being mistreated, I'd bring it home here to Noble Spirit to live the rest of its days in peace. Those animals got a right to that, at least."

I took the pot to the sink and poured water over the pile of peas until they floated gaily like bright green lily pads. When I set the pot on the stove, Mary put her floury hand on my forearm and said, "Why is it that you're the only one ever around when it's time to get the supper ready? Go on outside, now."

Out in the pasture, Jett, Flame, and Nacho stood in a row — side-by-side and nose to rump — brushing flies out of one another's eyes with their tails. It had grown cooler as the afternoon got later, and the no-see-ums were having a bug fiesta. The little black bastards sought out any moist orifice they could lay claim to, zooming straight for the eyes, ears, nose or mouth of any creature foolish enough to stand still for longer than ten seconds.

I went into the stable to make sure none of the horses got left in. We checked the horses over twice every day, after each meal. If a horse had a problem, he went into a stall to get cared for. Sometimes they needed salve on a cut or antibiotic ointment for an eye infection. At night we turned them out into the pasture to be together and live their regular horsy lives. Nobody picked on them anymore, or called them stupid or gay. Lucky them.

I wandered down the aisle of the barn looking into the stalls, my old beaten-up running shoes quiet on the pocked concrete. I heard a noise that made me stop and turn in a slow circle until I could figure out what it was and where it came from.

It was an animal sort of sound, and at first I thought one of the horses might be in trouble, but then I realized it wasn't like any animal I'd heard before. And it seemed to come from the stall at the far end of the barn. I walked toward it and sure enough the noise got louder.

I got to the stall door and went up on my tiptoes, so I could see in. Something was moving in the straw in the dark far corner, a snakelike writhing, and the noise continued. When I finally made sense of what I was seeing, I almost got sick right there. In the dim light, Graydon's bare bum waved like a white flag of surrender over Char's skinny body.

I ran back up to the house and refused to get anyone in for supper. Jerome got sent out to round everyone up, even though it was my turn.

"What's up with you?" asked Bobby G while we waited at the supper table for the others. "You look pale and flushed at the same time."

I looked at my belt buckle and shrugged.

So much for us all being careful of Graydon Fox. Char didn't waste any time, I gave her that at least. I shouldn't have been surprised.

"What's your story?" Graydon asked me.

It had been several days since I'd seen him and Char in their compromising position in the barn stall. I'd avoided him as much as I could. I hadn't met his gaze even once, and I think he was getting frustrated with me, since he couldn't figure out why. Out of the corner of my eye I could see him sometimes, dodging around, trying to get me to look at him.

We stood at the side of the stable, Graydon and Char aiming a garden hose at Twilight, a gentle black mare with a white star on her forehead, while I washed the top of Jett with a big yellow sponge and Tully washed his legs and underbelly.

"Ghost doesn't speak," said Tully, by way of response.

Graydon must have figured that out by now. In the corner of my eye, I caught him wink at me.

"She doesn't speak? Maybe she just needs a little persuasion."

"We leave each other alone here," said Tully, putting an arm protectively around my thighs. "It's not like Out There."

Tully said exactly what I was thinking, but I wanted to add that sometimes, only sometimes, it *was* like Out There, like when Jerome and Char got to calling each other nasty names. Mostly, though, the farm was better than Out There by a mile.

"This is your little sanctuary, is it, a paradise of peace and love? How nice."

His sarcasm brought a knot to my throat that ached fiercely.

The way Tully put it, saying that I don't speak, is probably pretty accurate. I used to speak; I have all the equipment in all the right places, anatomically. It wasn't like in those countries I'd read about, where a woman got her tongue cut out for gossiping or telling lies. I had a tongue but it had been more than two years since I'd used it for speaking.

And it wasn't like I had nothing to say. I had plenty to say. Sometimes, overwhelmed by how much speech I had in my head that wouldn't come out, I got dizzy and had to sit down. The words crowded together up behind my eyes. They gathered in my throat and I could see them as clear as daylight, dancing in my vision. But forcing the words through my mouth felt sort of like trying to suck a melon through a drinking straw. It was impossible to explain why, even to myself. It just didn't work. I couldn't put it all together, the words, my tongue, the sounds I wanted to make to tell the world my thoughts.

It hurt to want to speak so bad and not be able to, so I tried not to think too hard about what I wanted to say. I stayed away from conversations when I could, listening but not seen. I didn't want people to ask me questions. And trying to write down my answers hurt too, so I turned away from everyone until the questions stopped.

I preferred the horses. I hummed to them and they understood me without my having to say a word.

"Leave Ghost alone, right?" said Tully.

"Okay, okay." He flashed a beguiling smile and all at once I stopped being able to look away from him. "You don't have to get weird about it. I was just asking."

Graydon sprayed the stream of the hose on Char's bare legs. She shrieked and ran to the safety of the fence. Then he came at me, mischief dancing in his face, and waggled the end of the hose in front of him. I waved my arms in protest and backed away. I turned and a blast of cold water hit the back of my shorts and trickled down my legs into my shoes. The welcome chill of it on the hot afternoon thrilled me and I laughed out loud.

That was my first real laugh in two years, and I had Graydon Fox to thank for it.

"You kids quit messing around like that with them horses," Mary shouted from the side of the house, one hand on her huge hip. She must have heard me laugh because, despite the sternness in her voice, I saw her smile in my direction. I smiled back at her and carried my smile to Tully, who stood on the other side of the paddock fence. He didn't smile back at me and I let the grin wither.

I looked at Graydon, with his shaggy dark hair and misty eyes, which sometimes held a grey light in them, sometimes green and sometimes blue. I once had a mood ring like that. He had mood eyes, and I wished I could carry them around on my finger and look at them always.

Char stood at a safe distance, still laughing and almost doubled over.

I pitied Char for her ignorance and all the terrible things that had happened to her Out There on The Streets. Terrible things had happened to us all. I blamed her for having sex with Graydon. I felt a kind of nonspecific anger about it, but I also knew it was in Char's nature.

As for Graydon, he was a guy, like any other guy. The girls at school said all the sperm builds up, like the words in my head, until guys felt like they'd explode for want of relief.

No, I didn't blame him, mostly because I had somehow fallen in love with Graydon Fox.

Chapter 4

The sign at the road read "Noble Spirit Farm and Horse Sanctuary." I liked it there with Mary, Bobby and the horses. At all my previous foster homes, five in only three months, there had been too much noise and chaos. Most of the homes took in little kids and I was the only teenager, out of place and awkward.

A teenager entering the system for the first time tends to get bounced around a lot. The authorities didn't want to send me to a group home or halfway house, because of the bad influences. I hadn't committed a crime and they didn't want me to learn how. But foster homes for teenagers are kind of scarce. A lot of foster parents are looking for babies they can rescue and adopt, not nearly fully grown people that other parents have screwed up. So I had to bide my time at one place after another until a space opened up at a foster home that took in teenagers.

At the other places, I got treated like a retard, mostly. The foster parents spoke to me with deliberate slowness or ignored me completely. One foster mother made me go to Sunday school and baby-sit the little ones. She prayed and I tried to wipe orange Tang off their white T-shirts. At home, she spent her day watching religious television programs while I made sure no one drowned in the inflatable backyard pool.

As much as I loved this farm where I ended up, it was only a temporary stop. Mama was coming for me in the fall.

I had lived with my granny most of my life, because of Mama's problems, but Mama was going to be okay now. She was turning herself around and we'd live together like we were always meant to. Like other mothers and daughters live together. At the different foster homes, I used to sit with the other kids sometimes and watch reruns of this old show, *The Brady Bunch*. This perfect family. I pictured how, when we moved in together, Mama would let me watch her while she put on makeup, maybe even give me a lesson in mascara, and then we would wear each other's clothes and shoes.

Those were the times when I forgave her and imagined she forgave me. In fact, part of me believed we had already completely forgiven each other: me for being a burden and Mama for her terrible choices.

My memory was good. I remembered Mama's love from before things fell apart. I remembered the touch of her cool hand on my fevered forehead when flu raced through my body. I remembered the brush of her lips on my scraped knee just before she plastered a Band-Aid across it. No one should forget small mother comforts, Mary G once said. They become knitted through a soul, like roses embroidered on a piece of linen.

The problems for Mama and me began back in the time of gingham dresses, Raggedy Ann dolls and knee socks, even before Granny, when it was only us. It began with drinks of amber liquid in a brown-tinted glass shaped like the bottom of a pear.

Mama's face looked desolate, bleak eyes searched around me. I was there — small, perhaps three or four — but I wasn't.

After the drinks, Mama's limbs loosened, marionette-like, and her laughter grew loud and hollow, like an echo of happiness. I guess she was searching for some kind of comfort for herself that she couldn't get from me. She really wanted to be saved by a white knight.

Mama's boyfriend Morrow lived with us for a time. About his face I remember only his mouth. About his body I remember only his hands. Most of what I recall about him happened in the dark, on random nights, unpredictable and scary. Morrow's hands and mouth touched me. Through my pink flannel pyjamas with white clouds and grey elephants. The stink of his hands stayed after he had left my room. Musky cigarettes and sweet liquor. He shattered me. How many times? I couldn't remember.

Each time he whispered that if I told Mama, she wouldn't love me anymore. So, with no one to tell, no sister, no best friend, I began to wonder if it had happened at all. In the daytime he was jovial. He bought me stuffed animals and let me ride on his shoulders in a crowd.

The change came late one afternoon when I was five, Mama turned on the television and kissed the top of my head.

"We're going out, Annabel. You sit and watch some TV. We'll be back soon."

I got hungry when darkness fell and sat on the couch eating peanut butter out of the jar with my fingers, hoping Mama wouldn't be angry. I hadn't been able to find a slice of bread and the knives and spoons were all dirty in the sink.

I dragged a blanket from my bed to the couch and waited for Mama in a cold-sweat sleep that felt like someone else's fear.

The morning was quieter than any quiet I had ever heard. I shuffled to the bathroom and my pee hit the toilet water with the sound of thunder and the air in the apartment felt cold.

The TV droned on and on, with nothing to say, and no way to help me. Some of the hours that passed were daylight and some were night.

I remember the door bursting open and making my heart jump. I didn't know why the police hadn't knocked. I would have let them in.

I discovered later that the neighbours had heard me crying for hours, day and night from Friday afternoon to Sunday morning, and had called the police to release me.

I don't remember crying at all.

❧❧❧

On Canada Day afternoon at the farm, we dragged logs and bits of kindling out to the fire pit around the other side of the farmhouse. We had to keep the fire away from the horses. I didn't know if it was the crackle of the flames, the heat or the smell of the smoke that set them off, but Mary said horses would go crazy around fire.

Only Jerome had ever been camping, so he was kind of in charge. As for the rest of us, the annual Noble Spirit July First Barbecue and Bonfire was our one chance to melt the soles of our shoes and singe our faces to old campfire songs like *Row, Row, Row your Boat* (in rounds), *Kumbaya* and the one about not bringing your spectacles with you.

At mid-afternoon, Tully danced around the ring of stones, his hands barely reaching above his head.

"This is gonna be so much fun," he shouted. He loved junk like this and I couldn't help smiling at his child-like excitement. He got all of us caught up in his enthusiasm.

Bobby rolled the rusted-out barbecue next to the pit and Graydon helped him pull some old log benches and a rickety picnic table out of the shed. We propped dry logs into a pyramid in the middle of a circle of rocks, kindling all around it.

Tully and I were trying to push enough dirt under one of the legs of the warped picnic table to stop it from rocking while, sitting on the other side, Jerome acted as our violent-rocking-picnic-table tester. I anticipated potato salad getting dumped into someone's lap if we didn't fix the problem. Tully had just found a flat rock that might do the trick when Graydon marched straight up to the pit.

"It's ready." He whipped a lighter out of his jeans pocket and grabbed one of the pieces of newspaper Char had rolled up to start the fire.

"Not yet, Jerk-off," said Big Jerome, leaping up and knocking the lighter out of Graydon's hand before he had a chance to flick it on.

"Hey, what are you doing?" Ignoring the lighter that now lay in the dust, Graydon took a step forward until his chest almost touched Jerome's. They were nearly the same height (a bit shorter than me) but Jerome outweighed Graydon by at least fifty pounds. Despite Jerome's immense size, it was wiry Graydon who struck me with fear, his fists and teeth clenched tight, like an explosion was simmering in his skull.

"It's only four o'clock." Jerome's voice held less than his usual bravado. "If you light that fire now, there'll be nothing left of it by the time it gets dark." He gestured feebly around Graydon to the pile of sticks behind him.

"Don't ever touch me again," Graydon said.

"Hey, cool it, man. Why would I want to touch you anyway?" Jerome backed up.

Graydon stepped forward, which kept their chests tight together and made them look like unlikely dance partners. I wanted to step between them, tell them I loved them both.

Jerome was like a brother. If they went for each other, I didn't know who I'd root for.

I saw Jerome cover his testicles with his hands as Graydon darted around him and disappeared behind the corner of the house.

Jerome took off in the opposite direction, Char went after Graydon, and I picked the lighter out of the dirt, rubbed it clean on the hem of my T-shirt, and put it in my pocket.

"This is too much drama for me," Tully said, sighing like he was exhausted. We both went back to the table and I lifted it while he shoved the flat rock under its leg.

It worked. We got the picnic table level but no one else was around to notice.

Twenty minutes after she left, Char returned, crying but refusing to answer Tully's questions. My guess was that she tried to talk to Graydon and he told her to get lost. The one thing that their relationship was definitely not based on was meaningful conversation.

Jerome never missed a meal if he could help it. He slunk back before supper, subdued and quiet. We didn't see Graydon for hours.

When Bobby got the hamburgers and hotdogs all cooked up, Mary called for Graydon about a hundred times. She shook her head, wondering aloud where he was and why he hadn't shown up.

"Do any of you know what might've happened to Graydon?"

We were all lined up along the bench seats of the picnic table.

We shrugged, shook our heads, looked at our feet. Nobody said a word about what had happened. Even if I could have told, I wouldn't have. Mary put two hamburger patties and two hotdogs into a piece of tinfoil and kept them aside.

When the clouds of mosquitoes and black flies began to cluster around our heads in the relative cool of the summer evening, Bobby lit the bonfire. The wood, good and dry, caught quickly. Smoke billowed out, chasing the bugs into the gathering darkness.

Earlier, Tully, Jerome and I had each cut a long stick from the stand of skinny poplars that bordered one end of the pasture. We used them now to poke at the fire. I had cut one extra for Graydon and it lay at my side waiting for him.

"I wish my grandmother was here," said Jerome. "She loved a good fire."

I didn't exactly wish the same about my granny, but I nodded.

"Whenever we sat by the fire the old bat told the same story, an ancient legend of my people."

"I wish I had a People," Tully said.

The reflection of the fire in Tully's glasses obscured his eyes completely, and he looked like he had flames instead of eyes.

"No, you don't. Trust me," said Jerome. "It's too much responsibility."

"Tell us the story," said Tully.

"No. I don't remember it."

"Your grandmother told you this story every time you sat by a fire and you don't remember it? You do so. Tell it."

And Jerome began to tell the legend using his most Native voice, flat, yet lilting, mesmerizing. Roaring firelight heated our faces while night blackness cooled our backs.

"The Ojibwa people say that when the People came out of the ground — all People: the Bird People, the Animal People, the Insect People and the Human People — they opened their eyes and saw nothing."

"Bird People?" Tully giggled and waggled his stick, the glowing end of it dragging a temporary orange trail through the smoky air.

"Shut up. The world was dark, no sun, no moon, not even stars. The People moved around by touch, and if they found something that didn't eat them first, they ate it raw, for they had no fire to cook it. One day, all the People had a meeting. They decided that living in the dark was too cold and miserable and they had to find a solution. A voice rang out, 'The People in the East have fire!' According to rumour, fire gave warmth and light, and they decided they should have it too. From the dark came another voice, 'But the People from the East are greedy. They won't share fire with us.' The People decided they would steal the fire."

Jerome pushed at a log with his stick and it fell, showering the flames with fresh sparks.

"Grandmother Spider volunteered, 'I'll do it. Let me try!' But her voice was drowned out by Beaver, 'I, Beaver, great chief of animals, will go to the East, take the fire, and hide it in the bushy hair on my tail.' At that time Beaver had the widest, flattest, and furriest tail of all the animals, so it was agreed.

"Beaver went to the East and found the beautiful orange fire, jealously guarded. Beaver got closer and closer, until he grabbed a burning stick and shoved it into the bushy hair on his flat tail. Immediately, his tail went up in flames, and all the people of the East saw Beaver stealing their fire. They took back the fire and drove Beaver away. Every bit of hair had been burned from Beaver's tail and, to this day, beavers have no hair at all on their tails.

"Beaver had failed. 'Let *me* go. I can do it!' cried Grandmother Spider once again, but this time they chose Crow, for Crow was very clever. At that time, Crow was pure white and had the most beautiful song of all the birds. But he took so long standing over the fire in the East, trying to decide which piece was best to steal, the smoke turned his white feathers black. And he breathed in so much smoke, his beautiful song came out as a harsh, 'Caw, Caw.' The people of the East drove Crow away as well.

"Tiny Grandmother Spider shouted as loud as she could, 'Let me try, *please!*' The others thought she had little chance of success, but it was agreed she could have a turn. Grandmother Spider walked to a river nearby. Out of the clay from the riverbank, she made a small pot and a lid with a notch in it for air. She put the container on her back and spun a web all the way to the East and walked tiptoe until she came to the fire. She was so small that the people didn't notice her, and so she took a tiny piece of fire, put it into the container, and closed the lid. Then she walked back along the web until she came home to the People. They couldn't see any fire, so they groaned, 'Grandmother Spider has failed.'

"She said, 'Oh no, I have the fire.' She lifted the lid of the pot and the fire flamed up into its friend, the air. The Bird People looked at poor black Crow and decided they didn't want the fire. The Animal People looked at poor Beaver and decided they didn't want the fire. But the Human People stepped forward, 'We'll take it,' they said.

"So Grandmother Spider taught the Human People how to feed the fire with wood to stop it from dying and how to keep the fire safe in a circle of stone so it couldn't escape and hurt them or their homes."

His grandmother's story finished, Jerome paused.

"I don't know how much of that is real Ojibwa legend, and how much my grandmother made up. She was kind of a kooky old bird in her old age."

"Well, that sucked." Graydon was standing behind us, smiling, his teeth flashing ghostly in the firelight.

"You suck," said Jerome without turning around. His tone was too weary to invite a fight. I handed Graydon the stick I had cut for him, and he walked around the circle and sat on a log across the pit from the rest of us.

Tully yawned. "I'm going to bed." He got up off his log bench and walked toward the lights of the farmhouse.

We sat in silence for a time, watching the embers glow orange and yellow, waxing and waning, sighing into the night air. I got lost in their beauty and power, imagining the story of the small spider escaping with the fire contained in her little pot.

Graydon was suddenly bending down beside me and holding out his palm. "Come with me," he breathed into my hair.

Before I left the warmth of the circle of fire, I leaned down and kissed Jerome on the cheek. In surprise, his chubby hand slapped the spot I had kissed and he looked up. I smiled at him, put a steadying hand on his shoulder, and stepped over the log benches into the cool night.

Graydon's palm was hot in mine as he pulled me along behind him. I felt the eyes of Jerome and Char against my back. I thought I heard Char mumble a bitter, "Good riddance," but I didn't look back at them.

I expected Graydon to take me into one of the stable stalls, like he had done with Char. If he tried to do that, I planned to resist, punch him, and run off. I was not Char. But instead we went into the darkness of the woods that bordered the east side of the property. I shivered, less with the cold than anticipation.

He led me to an apple tree whose thick, twisting branches formed a seat low to the ground and wide enough for us to sit on.

Nervous, I stared out into the dark. Tiny blinking lights danced through the air. I pointed at them and looked at Graydon. I gasped. One of the lights had got caught in the front of his hair and it winked like a feeble yellow strobe light. I cupped my palms and slowly eased them around the light until I had it trapped in my hands. In the space between my thumbs, the little lightning bug went on and off. Graydon's head bent next to mine and I felt his hair brush against my forehead.

"Wow. Cool. I've never seen a firefly before."

I opened my hands and it winked into its freedom before it disappeared.

Graydon put his arm around my shoulders.

"I like you, Annabel."

Startled, I pulled back to face him.

"I found out your real name from Char. She knew it. I think it's very pretty, just like you."

It annoyed me that he used my old name, but I felt pleased that he liked me. I settled back against the crook of his arm and let him place a hand on my bare thigh.

"You're not jealous of Char, are you?"

I shook my head but I hadn't completely decided if I was jealous. I blamed her for seducing him, but jealousy was a different story. Maybe I was jealous.

"You shouldn't be. You're a very special girl. Char's just a whore who doesn't know anything except fucking."

I squirmed at the harshness of the words he was whispering, like tenderness, in my ear.

"Sorry, but that's just how I see it."

The hand on my thigh brushed up my arm and onto my cheek. Gently, he turned my head toward his face and pressed his lips to mine. It was a dry sort of kiss, but soft. He smelled of bug spray and leftover mango-scented sunscreen.

I pulled out of the kiss before he did.

"That was nice," he said.

I hopped off the tree branch, stuck my hands into my shorts' pockets and walked back to the house without looking back. I didn't know what he thought of me for doing that.

I went to bed with the stink of wood smoke in my hair, the words of a grandmother's fire legend in my head and the trace of Graydon's kiss on my lips.

Chapter 5

My birthday came around in early August. As it neared, I thought more about home, Mama and Granny. Granny had always been a hard woman, from the tightness of her worm-like lips to her stiff, sensible shoes.

"Annabel, you're capable of so much more," she would say to me every time I handed her my report card.

Her expectations were a rock tied around my neck. I'm sure the expectations weighed down Mama, too, most of her life, but she had managed to escape by running away. Considering the way things went, though, her so-called escape was more like 'out of the frying pan and into the fire'.

Of all the birthdays I could remember from my childhood, Mama was present at two: my seventh and my tenth. I had a pretty good recollection of my tenth, sitting on the saggy green couch in the living room of Granny's apartment, waiting to see if Mama would come.

Granny didn't like other children — I'm not sure she cared for me all that much — so I wasn't allowed to have a party. Granny winced at the thought of the noise and mess a bunch of ten-year-olds might make, her lips pressed together tighter than ever. She believed parties were self-indulgent. If Mama didn't come to visit, birthdays passed entirely without fanfare. I didn't know when Granny's birthday even was, and she wouldn't tell me.

The idea of Mama walking through the apartment door made my skin prickle with sweat and my head feel light. I feared her coming as much as I yearned for her to come. It was like staring at a facedown poker hand with all your money in the pot. Picking it up might mean losing everything. Or it could mean hitting the jackpot.

I sat on the green couch, trying to read a teen magazine, but the words floated around, refusing to make any sort of sense. Sweat soaked the back of my T-shirt and shorts and I had to change into fresh clothes.

"Why don't you get up and go outside?" Granny needled at me. "It's a beautiful day and you look like you could use the air."

"No thanks. I'm a little tired today."

"Are you waiting for that mama of yours? Because I'm sure she's not coming, and even if she does come, it'll be all the worse for you."

"No, I'm not waiting. I'm just tired."

"Fine. Let your young muscles atrophy there on that couch. You won't appreciate how strong you are until you get old like me."

Granny was forty-four when she had Mama. Mama had me when she was eighteen. Granny was the oldest person I'd ever met. Everything about her was old, from her clothes to her attitude. Being young around her was hard.

At about two in the afternoon, the doorknob turned and there stood Mama. She never announced herself by buzzing up. She always waited until she could scoot in through the door behind a tenant. Granny, in the only motherly gesture I can remember, let Mama keep a key to our apartment. Maybe she was more optimistic about Mama than I thought she was. She definitely ended up being more naïve.

My disappointment was complete the moment I saw Mama. She shambled over the threshold, the handles of a grocery bag looped over one wrist and juggling a small cardboard box. Her legs, clad in tight denim shorts, looked so thin there was a space between them even at her crotch.

Her eyes, black with pupil, seemed to whirl around in her face and a strand of dark hair was caught in the corner of her mouth. She came into the living room shuffling her feet against the floor, to keep her flip-flops on.

"Annabel."

"Hi Mama."

"Is your granny here?" she asked, in a low voice, bending almost double at the waist.

"Crystal." Granny came through from the kitchen and stood right beside Mama.

"Oh, hi Mom."

The box in Mama's hand looked like it was about to fall. Granny took it from her and set it on the dining table.

"A little something for the birthday girl." Mama smiled.

I smiled back and dug my fingernails into my palms, feeling them bite.

"Crystal, do you have to come here, like this?"

"Don't start." Mama sighed and pressed her fingertips to her temples.

"Well, you'll be pleased to know that I'm going out for an hour. I'll leave you two alone."

"Sorry to hear you won't be joining us on Annabel's birthday, Mom."

"I'm sure you are. You have an hour." Granny turned to me. "I'll be at Olga's."

Olga was Granny's only friend. She lived in the apartment below ours with about a hundred cats and her place stank something fierce. I always had to struggle to understand the English underneath her strong accent. Sometimes she and Granny would have a fight and Granny would storm upstairs vowing never to speak to her again. But right the next day, there she'd be, heading down to Olga's for afternoon tea.

Granny put on a pair of slip-on shoes and went out the door without a second glance at Mama.

"How's my girl?" asked Mama.

"Fine. How are you?"

"I'm doing real good." She flung off the flip-flops and walked over to the couch, each step planted carefully, as if she were avoiding stepping on cockroaches all over the floor. "You want to sit outside?"

"Sure."

We went to the balcony and Mama pulled a fresh pack of cigarettes out of the grocery bag she still carried. She struggled for a moment with the wrapping, her fingers trembling, and handed the pack to me with a shrug. I pulled the tab of the cellophane and opened it for her, shoving the wrapper into my pocket to throw out later.

"Thanks."

She stuck a cigarette between her lips and lit it with a pink lighter. I sat on one of two lawn chairs and Mama stood at the railing, her knee pumping in a frenzy, and smoked.

"How are you getting along here, with your granny?"

"Fine, Mama."

"How's school?"

"It's good. I got an A in English on my final report card."

"I'll bet you did. Take after me. I always got pretty good marks in English. What did Granny say to that, the sour-faced old bitch?"

The curse was a slap across my cheek, but I smiled anyway. It was like Mama and me against Granny, like we were on the same side in an ongoing battle.

"Nothing much."

"I got you a cake there, for your birthday. What are you now, nine?"

"I'm ten today." The feeling of being on the same side fell away and my fingernails dug troughs in my palms.

"Right, ten."

"You want to have some cake with me?"

"No, thanks. I'm not hungry, and your grandmother would kill me if I took this cigarette into the house."

"Yeah, she's like psychic or something. She knows everything."

Mama finished lighting another cigarette with the end of the first and laughed, but there was no humour in it.

"She sure does."

Mama was quiet for a time. One arm wrapped around her body, the elbow of her other arm resting on her wrist, the cigarette poised beside her cheek.

From the tree that separated our apartment building from the one next to it came a ping-ping-ping cry, like the sound of a video game laser gun. I looked through the branches and finally spotted it in the large pine. A cardinal, brilliant red and singing with the joy of its freedom, a crimson decoration on an otherwise bare Christmas tree.

"Listen, Annabel," said Mama, finally. "I'm trying to sort things out, you know. I've got a new boyfriend now, Greg, and he's a good guy. He says you can come and live with us when we get things settled. We're working on getting enough money together to rent a nice place with an extra bedroom, for you."

I wanted to believe her like I had never wanted anything. "That would be great." I knew she wanted me as much as I wanted her. I didn't care about this unknown Greg. He'd be gone eventually, like all the others, and that would leave Mama and me. If she could only quit the drugs I was sure everything would be perfect.

"It would be great, wouldn't it? We could paint the walls of your room pink. I know how you like pink. You could bring all your stuffed animals. Greg could make us breakfast every morning, scrambled eggs and sausages."

She was on a roll now. I decided not to interrupt and tell her I didn't like pink anymore, I had sold all my stuffed animals in a garage sale, and remind her that she never, ever, ate breakfast.

Mama stopped talking and I searched the branches of the tree for the cardinal but it had flown away.

"I should go. You know, before your granny gets back."

"Don't go, Mama." I struggled to stop myself from grabbing her around the knees.

"I have to." She looked out at the apartment building beyond the tree. "I can't see my mother again, I just can't."

She flicked the last cigarette butt over the railing to join the three others and walked back into the apartment.

"Take care of yourself. I'll call you."

"Bye, Mama. Thanks for coming."

"I wouldn't miss your birthday."

And then she was gone.

I went into my tiny bedroom, bit my pillow, and screamed.

⬦⬦⬦

As my fifteenth birthday loomed, I had trouble sleeping. I knew I could count on Mary to do something special but I refused to get my hopes up about having a good birthday, out of habit, I suppose.

On the fifth of August, Mary and Bobby woke me with a cake. By that I mean I woke up to Mary standing over my bed holding a home-baked cake with fifteen candles ablaze. Behind her Bobby, Tully, Char and Jerome drew a collective breath and began a tuneless version of *Happy Birthday*.

Why wasn't Graydon there? I knew he didn't like to get up early, but I'd hoped he would make an exception for my birthday. Maybe the others had decided not to tell him, to exclude him on purpose, out of jealousy or something. But I knew Mary wouldn't be in on something like that. She would've told him in advance, and woken him up in time to join them.

I blew out the candles to a smattering of applause.

"Happy Birthday, Ghost," said Mary.

"Let's go down to the kitchen so we can cut the cake," said Tully, rubbing his small hands together. He adored anything sweet. "I love birthdays around here. Whoever heard of cake for breakfast?"

The cake was chocolate and rich as pudding. I'd helped to bake cakes for other birthdays. At Mary's house, everyone got up super early on someone's birthday morning, sneaked down to the kitchen, and baked a cake before the birthday person got out of bed.

Each of us was finishing a second piece, when Char stood. "I'll go first." And one by one, they presented me with small gifts, bought with money from the slim weekly allowance Mary managed to afford to dole out.

Char gave me an electric toothbrush, Jerome a glittering piece of polished quartz, and Tully a thin book of inspirational poems. Mary handed me a small package and said, "This is from Bobby and me. It isn't much."

Inside the wrapping was another book: *The United States Pony Club Manual of Horsemanship*.

"Bobby and me, we both think you have a real way with the horses. It'd be a shame to waste it. I wish we could get you a horse to ride and some proper lessons, but that isn't in the cards, or the bank account, at the moment. I thought you could read up on it, though, for now."

I pulled the book to my chest with one arm and with the other hugged Mary and then Bobby. It wasn't just the book; it was that they thought enough of me to give it.

Even in the midst of the embrace, I couldn't help glancing through the kitchen window over Bobby's shoulder. Where was Graydon? What could he have been up to? Why was I always waiting for something?

My only real sadness that morning arose because I hadn't been able to share the cake or the moment with Graydon.

Chapter 6

Still early on my birthday morning, even before the horses had travelled down to the paddock from the field, I came out of the barn with a wheelbarrow full of muck and saw Bobby and Jerome heading for the workshop. Jerome walked behind, trying to get his feet to step squarely in each of Bobby's boot prints. If he'd known I was watching, he'd have stopped doing it. Any time I couldn't find Jerome all I had to do was look for Bobby and there he was. Jerome had latched onto Bobby like an imprinted duckling, following him everywhere that Bobby allowed him to.

Bobby helped Mary and us kids look after the horses on the farm, but he was a carpenter by trade. During the school year, which was coming up fast, he also worked as a shop teacher at a nearby high school.

I dumped the muck out of the wheelbarrow and walked over to the doorway of Bobby's shed, beyond the big hay barn. Peering in, I saw all the familiar junk: a jigsaw and lathe, planes and sanders, both manual and electric, and all manner of woodworking contraptions that probably had names, but I didn't know them. I couldn't tell what the floor of the shed was made of because I'd never seen it. It was always covered in curls of light-yellow wood and heaps of sawdust.

I liked the natural smell of new-cut pine and cedar, but didn't care for the noise of the machines or the lung-clogging thickness of the air inside the shed. If I went there at all, I preferred to hang around in the fresh air outside the doorway, looking in. Bobby and Jerome had got to work quickly. They had on identical geeky plastic goggles that protected their eyes from flying chunks of wood, and white masks that made them look like surgeons.

When I watched people doing what they loved to do, in those quiet moments of joy, like Tully and Char at the Reading Rock, I felt content too. I heard the whine of a machine starting up. In a few minutes, Bobby and Jerome had a layer of wood dust over their work clothes. Jerome's black hair, which hung past his shoulders and was done up in a ponytail, was blond with dust. Jerome looked toward the door and I raised my hand in a wave. His hands were out of sight and busy, so he just nodded to me. He probably smiled, too, but I couldn't see his mouth for the mask. I wandered back to the stable.

Although he protected himself fiercely by insulting and putting down other people, Jerome wasn't afraid to share a lot of intimate information. He could be utterly frank and matter-of-fact about the most disturbing incidents from his past and would tell them without a hint of discomfort or embarrassment. I figured he enjoyed the shock value.

I glanced back at the shed and imagined them inside it, Jerome and Bobby side by side. Jerome had told me his own daddy hadn't been much of a father to him. He said his mother and father drank and fought and ignored him and his little brother, unless they made trouble. Then they got the back of his father's hand across their faces.

"When things got rough at home," he said, "my parents sent George and me to our grandmother's house for a month or two at a time. That wasn't so bad. My grandmother was a pretty cool lady, with all her stories and junk. She showed us some of the old ways and talked about the legends. George ate it up. He loved all that crap. She got old, though, and couldn't take us anymore."

Jerome's father was a hunter and kept all kinds of guns in a case in their living room. But the drinking made him careless.

"My dad left a goddamn gun lying around one day and my stupid little brother picked it up. I walked into my parents' bedroom. I saw him standing with the gun. It felt like I was one of those cartoon characters, where their legs run in place but their body doesn't go anywhere, you know? I stood there like that, running to stop him but not getting anywhere. But then I heard the shot. And saw the blood. I didn't know a little body could have so much freaking blood."

Six-year-old George had died instantly and Jerome got whisked away to Noble Spirit.

Everyone had a story.

⬦⬦⬦

I thought fifteen would feel different, that I'd be transformed somehow. I guess it was one of those hopes that would never happen — to wake up a different person. Maybe people wanted to be whatever they weren't, like a grass-is-always-greener kind of thing. Char wished she could read; Jerome wanted to shed twenty pounds; and Tully longed to be bigger and tougher. I wanted the best parts of all of them to become part of me: Char's confidence, Jerome's kindness, Tully's gentleness. Maybe that's why I liked to watch them, unobserved.

After I mucked out the stalls I fed the horses because it was my turn. Birthday or not, horses had to eat.

Healthy, contented horses didn't need to be told twice when their food was ready. Several expectant heads already hung over the fence, watching me and waiting. After I poured grain into their buckets and pans, and placed them on the ground, I opened the gate and let the animals into the paddock from the pasture.

Nacho, a miniature horse small even by miniature horse standards, was munching away when I noticed a gash on his right hindquarter. Blood had congealed and hardened in a dark streak under the cut. It looked like he had snagged his little rump on a wire or sharp branch. I waited until he finished eating and took him into a stall to wait for Mary or Bobby to come down to the barn and take a look.

Mary told me Nacho had been severely abused by a man who tried to train him to pull a cart. He would scream at Nacho, beating him with a whip, a crop, a stick or whatever came to hand, until he bled. Nacho came to Noble Spirit without a spirit at all. Several years ago, whenever Mary approached him, his body trembled and he peed straight down his hind legs. I didn't understand how anyone could do that to an animal, especially one they were supposed to care for.

Now I could put a hand on the little horse, provided he saw me coming. If I made a sudden movement, or touched him without making sure he knew I was there, he would bolt to the far fence line, legs shaking and chest heaving.

As I moved off to check the other horses, I spotted Graydon standing on the bottom fence rail.

"Happy birthday," he shouted.

I felt an embarrassed rush of blood sweep into my cheeks.

"Come here, Birthday Girl," he said, "I have something to show you."

I let him help me over the fence, even though I didn't need his help, and he took my hand. He led me into the hay barn. Strips of late-morning light stretched across the dirt floor, straw dust drifting between the shadows. Earthy smells of fusty hay and wet leather.

Graydon went ahead and sat on one of several bales that had been arranged in a square. He placed a finger over his lips and then, with the same finger, pointed down into the hole among the bales.

When I got close enough, I saw them, a litter of kittens, no more than a day old. The fat tabby mother that Tully had named Sacha lay stretched out beside a jumble of tiny sleeping bodies. Each of the mother's slit eyes revealed a shred of luminescent green. Graydon reached down and grasped a kitten. Sacha watched with bland interest.

The kitten's tiny football-shaped head, ears pressed flat, eyes tight shut, had a pink swirl of a nose the size of a nail head. It mewled blindly, impulsive and instinctual. Its front legs splayed outward over the top of Graydon's fist, the pink pads of its paws nestled together like pieces in a jigsaw puzzle. The cone of its stunted tail stuck straight out.

I laughed in delight, the sound of it jangling through the barn like someone kicking a tin can full of rocks. I clamped my hand over my mouth and laughed again. Graydon placed the kitten in my lap, where it wormed and bobbed. I scooped it up carefully, lifted it to my face and let its fine baby fur tickle my lips.

"I've been watching the mother," he said in a low voice. "I could tell she was going to have those kittens soon. I followed her around yesterday, to see where she'd choose. I caught her going into Bobby's workshop and, after she had them last night, I put them all in a blanket and carried them here instead. I thought the noise of him working might stress out the kittens. She was really good about it. Didn't try to scratch me or anything, just let me move the bunch of them."

Graydon was cool and handsome and had that weird energy that made me tingle, but I hadn't imagined he could be thoughtful or caring. I put the kitten back in the hay with its mother and hugged Graydon's arm to my chest. I knew the gesture was awkward, I wasn't used to hugging, but it felt right to do it. To thank him for giving me this birthday moment with him.

He pulled back a few moments later and looked at me. "Are you happy?"

I nodded and smiled.

"I'm glad," he said. "I wish I could hear your voice, even once."

I wished it too.

We watched the kittens jostle each other for nipple space.

"They look like commuters trying to get to a bank of pay phones at an airport," Graydon said, and I laughed.

Some of the babies had tabby markings like Sacha, but some were pure black, I assumed like their father. We didn't have another cat at the farm so she must have wandered to find her mate, or sow her wild oats, or whatever you're supposed say about females who sleep around. Animals were such an obvious combination of mother and father, of egg and sperm.

After a time, we left the kittens and their mama in peace.

⊷⊷⊷

I was lounging on the living room couch reading a book when I heard Mary holler my name from the laundry room.

When I went in, she turned to me and held out Graydon's plastic lighter.

"Ghost, I found this in your pocket."

My head hung. I hadn't done anything particularly wrong, but felt a vague guilt just the same.

"I'm gonna ask you straight out. Are you smoking?"

I gave her my most earnest look and shook my head.

"Okay. You haven't ever given me cause to doubt you, so I won't this time either." She handed the lighter back to me. "I don't want a reason to be disappointed in my Ghost, you hear me?"

I nodded and turned back to the living room. Graydon stood in the doorway. I showed him the lighter that I'd plucked from the ground that day after the fight. I wasn't sure if he knew I'd had it since then, but he shrugged a slight apology anyway, for his lighter getting me into trouble, and I shrugged an it's-okay back at him. I didn't want to give the lighter to him in front of Mary, for fear he'd catch trouble way worse than I had, so I kept it with me.

⌁⌁⌁

Tully chose my room to sleep in that night and I lay listening to the rhythmic breath of his not-quite-asleep body beside me.

The puffs of the wind through the gap in my open window whispered of the autumn coolness that would soon come, so I was grateful for Tully's warmth.

"Ghost, I've been thinking about what Jerome said, about the responsibility of having a People. I don't agree with him." Tully's small voice was strong, more awake than his breathing had suggested. "I don't think having a People would be too much responsibility at all. I think knowing where you came from would give you a real sense of who you are and where you might be going."

I knew where I came from, and if my past told me anything, it wasn't anything good.

"Sometimes I imagine being able to see a face that looks like mine. To hear words like, 'He's just like Uncle Joe,' or 'His chin is like his father's.' My God, that would be beautiful."

For what it was worth, I looked like Granny. Even her being so old and me being so young, I could see the resemblance. I didn't look much like Mama, not even when she was my age. A small piece of me wanted to know what my father looked like. I thought of the kittens Graydon had shown me in the barn, how some looked exactly like the mother, but others were so different. I wondered what about me might have come from my father and the thought made me sad. Maybe the part of my face that wasn't Granny's was his. Maybe the way I held a spoon, or how I buttered my toast, were his ways. These things I would never know. Dwelling on them was heartache. But Tully couldn't help himself.

"I want a family, Ghost, and if I'm doomed to grow up without one, I'll darn well make one for myself when I get Out There, no matter how hard it is."

Granny had kept a picture of her late husband on one of the side tables in the living room. His handsome but stern face, disapproving, looked out at everything we did. His first name had been Thomas and I wondered if Granny had called him Tom. I never got a chance to call him anything because he was already dead when I was born, which was good since my out-of-wedlock birth would probably have killed him anyway. It damn near killed Granny.

Would he have been Grandpa, Grandpop, Grandad, Pappy? As it was, he was simply my dead grandfather. He'd been an orthopedic surgeon and I could tell from his photograph he had overwhelmed everyone in his presence with expectations. While he was alive and earning bags of money, Granny and Mama wanted for nothing except his approval. He looked like he would have been stingy with that, stingier even than Granny, which was saying something.

Mama didn't speak about him. If he was mentioned, she called him The Bastard, which made Granny go mental. I assumed that was why Mama said it, but maybe he had been a bastard.

Family could be a slippery concept. Granny and Mama were my blood family, but neither really treated me in the way I imagined family should treat a child. Mary was the kind of mother I would have picked for myself, if I had been given the choice. If, on the day of my birth, God Himself had hovered before me on a set of silver wings and said, "Child, you can choose for yourself, from among the millions of mamas on the great planet earth," I felt certain I would have chosen Mary Gervais.

The fact was, I knew where I came from and wished I didn't.

"Ghost?"

I jerked my head toward Tully, like I was impatient for him to stop talking and leave me to sleep, but I wasn't.

"I know that you come to the Reading Rock and that you listen to me reading the stories to Char."

I started to shake my head in protest.

"It's okay. I like it. It makes me read better." He hesitated. "Having you around makes everything better."

A balloon grew large in my chest and a tear ran from the corner of one eye into my ear. I wiped it away with my shoulder.

"Happy birthday, Ghost."

❧❧❧

I'm riding Jett, feeling the strength of his muscles between my long, bare legs. Mama, who is sober and shining, rides beside me on Twilight. She smiles and reaches toward me. I put out my hand and she takes it, squeezes it in hers. She laughs.

Pollen drifts in the heat of a summer day and we ride along a narrow trail into the woods, and Mama's horse pulls ahead of mine. The mottled shadows of light and dark dapple Twilight's hindquarters and swishing tail while she rocks and sways between the trees.

Twilight begins to trot, but I can't make Jett go faster. Mama swivels to look back at me, still smiling. She waves and turns away. Twilight breaks into a canter. I jab Jett hard with my heels but he stops. He's standing still now and I can see Twilight and Mama disappearing, swallowed by the trees, which now gather closer to me, pulling darkness in.

I want to yell for Mama to stop. Wait. But I can't make a sound. I try to get off Jett and run after Mama on foot, but the trees have closed in and are tangled around my ankles, holding me in place.

A scream strangles me.

◦⊸◦⊸◦

I woke in the same position I had fallen asleep in, lying in fever-sweat darkness, smelling the night air. Why was it so hot?

I held my breath for a moment but somehow kept breathing. No, that wasn't me. I had forgotten that Tully had crept in and now lay on the other side of the bed.

He arched and writhed beneath the sheet that covered us both. I wondered if he was having a nightmare too. I almost reached out to waken him.

His profile reflected moonlight, his lips slightly parted; he moaned. Then I knew what he was doing.

I thought of dirty Morrow in my bed, with his hands and mouth. I could almost smell his scent of cigarettes and liquor.

But Tully smelled of toothpaste and oranges and touched only himself. It was embarrassing to be right there beside him, so I lay still and pretended to be asleep. I tried not to listen until he finally stopped, rolled over and fell into a sighing sleep.

Chapter 7

Mama's worst choices always involved men. Every time she visited me at Granny's, which was only a few times a year, she had a new boyfriend. She brought one or two to the apartment to meet me. They all arrived high, like Mama. Granny usually threw the guys out almost before they got through the door, and then barely tolerated Mama for the following hour or so. Mama's desire not to piss off the latest boyfriend made her visits short. The guy waited outside for her, if she was lucky, and she twitched and stole glances at the clock the whole time.

I remember the first day I met Julian. I had come home from school early because it was the start of the Christmas holidays, and I felt pretty pleased to dump grade seven for a couple of weeks.

Granny stood in the kitchen, pounding at, mixing, or chopping something. She loved to bake and cook, and she was good at both too. She could cook anything from beef Wellington to jambalaya.

"What are you doing home so early?" she asked.

"It's Christmas vacation," I said.

"So they can't teach you to the end of the day? Two weeks out of school isn't enough for them, they have to send you home early too."

I shrugged and took a few home baked chocolate chip cookies from the jar on the counter.

"You had better get your homework done then."

"But Granny, it's Christmas break. I have two whole weeks to do it."

"You'd rather wait to the last minute and scramble as usual?"

I sighed because I knew I wouldn't win the argument. When Granny wielded her huge guilt-stick, she smote me every time.

I got my backpack from the hallway and dumped my dog-eared duotangs and schoolbooks onto the kitchen table. My grade seven teacher worked us like pack mules. He seemed to love giving additional homework whenever possible and took advantage of the extra-long break by handing out assignments during the last week of school. I lined up my work in the order I wanted to do it, easiest first, and hunkered down.

I didn't mind homework because I did well in school, in most subjects. Math sometimes baffled me, but anything that involved reading or writing came easy. So my books were arranged like this: English book report on *A Tree Grows in Brooklyn*, which I had already read on my own the year before and loved, social studies report on Indonesia, an essay about Louis Riel, and finally algebra.

I had finished the English book report and was moving on to social studies when the apartment door squeaked open.

Granny and I turned to each other and listened, a tableau of anticipation.

"Hello? Anybody home?" came Mama's too-cheery voice from the hall.

We got up and walked out of the kitchen, and there stood Mama with her hand in the back pocket of an emaciated man. He wore ripped jeans and a denim jacket that was far too light for the weather.

"Mom, Annabel, this is Julian," she said, as proudly as if she were introducing a school valedictorian.

Granny's lips had all but disappeared as she stared at her daughter and the latest boyfriend.

"Hi Mama," I said.

"Hi Sweets."

Julian raised a dirty hand in greeting and jogged his knees up and down while his gaze raced all over the apartment.

"I'm sorry I can't invite you in," said Granny. "Annabel is right in the middle of her homework."

"Oh, Mom. It's almost Christmas. Give the kid a break."

"Annabel lives with me, Crystal. I decide what she does, and when she does it."

I wanted to protest because it sounded like I was some kind of puppet, but Granny was right. She did decide.

In the absence of an invitation to enter, Mama and Julian stood in the front hall, sheep waiting to be led one way or another.

"I have a present for Annabel," said Mama, holding a plastic grocery bag tied in a knot at the top.

"How thoughtful," said Granny, taking the bag before I had a chance to step forward.

Granny stood with the handle loops of the plastic bag around one wrist, her hands clasped in front of her. We waited for something to happen.

"I guess the old hag isn't gonna invite us in," said Julian.

"I beg your pardon?" Granny said, rising to the balls of her feet. "This is my house and you have come here unannounced, and stoned to boot. I'm not going to give you money, Crystal, so you and your charming friend can go along home now, if you have one." Round red spots had risen high on Granny's wrinkly cheeks.

I wanted to speak up, to say I was desperate to spend time with my mother, but Julian, sharp-angled in his skinniness, had a dangerous edge to him that made me stay far back and say nothing. I had hoped Mama would tell him to wait outside so she could visit with me, but she didn't.

"All right, Mother. We'll go. Merry Christmas."

"Same to you," said Granny, reaching around Mama to grab the doorknob and usher them out.

"Bye sweetie," Mama said over her shoulder. "See you soon."

I said goodbye and then Mama and Julian were gone. I rolled my bottom lip between my teeth and looked at a speck of dirt on the carpet, until I felt the soft warmth of Granny's palm across the back of my neck.

"We'll put this under the tree, shall we?"

I nodded and watched Granny's feet move away toward the fake Christmas tree that sat on a table in the corner of the apartment by the window. It shed thin green strips of paper or fabric (I couldn't tell what it was made of) that clung to the baseboards with static electricity. They were difficult to vacuum up and I found them wedged between the wall and carpet long into summer.

"That's enough homework for now, Annabel. I'll clear your books off the table for you, and you can go and do whatever you please until dinner."

I felt like vomiting, but instead I went to my room and lay on my bed until Granny called me to the table to eat.

I didn't think I'd see Julian again. Most of my mother's boyfriends didn't last long enough to make a second visit to Granny's apartment.

~◦~◦~◦~

On Christmas Eve, only days after I had met Mama's new boyfriend, I woke up before dawn to the guilty realization I hadn't bought Granny a Christmas gift.

Without a thought in my head of what I'd buy, I wrote a note for Granny that I'd gone out. I folded it and propped it against the sugar bowl on the kitchen table. I got dressed and went down to the corner to catch the bus to the local mall.

I barely got settled into a seat at the back of the bus before trouble found me. Three girls from my school climbed on at the next stop. Mackenzie, Morgan and Taylor were responsible for a lot of student misery. They must have put a bunch of girls on a future psychiatrist's couch. So many, they'd probably get a kickback someday.

Morgan wore a snow-white bomber jacket, Taylor a short black wool coat, Mackenzie a fur-trimmed shiny black number. They looked so fashionable I felt self-conscious in my puke green ski jacket with dirt ground into sleeves that were an inch too short. I tried to hide by pulling the collar higher over my jaw. Of course, they spotted me.

"If it isn't Anus Bell," Morgan said. "How's your anus today, Bell?" The other two laughed and they all squeezed into the seat across the aisle from me. I looked away — out through the grime-encrusted bus window, out at the filthy sidewalk whipping past — and hoped they would do the same. They didn't.

"Your Mama give you any drugs lately that you'd like to share with the rest of the class?"

"Leave me alone, Taylor. Please." I didn't look at them.

"Leave you alone? What fun would that be?"

Their mothers probably took them shopping at lingerie stores and paid for their manicures, shining shell pink on their pudgy tween fingers. They had never seen some of the things I had seen. I was jealous of their smooth, carefree faces.

I was always unpopular at school but I didn't have the vaguest idea why. When I looked at myself in the mirror, I didn't see anything obvious to set me apart. Although I was a bit shy, I could speak; the teen blemishes on my face were few; it seemed to me that my body looked okay; I didn't have to wear four-eyes glasses or tinsel-teeth braces. Nevertheless, I went to class, studied in the library and went home, never getting invited to parties that I knew were being planned around me.

Patrick was the only guy who hung out with me. He was in worse shape, popularity-wise, than I was. His hair flamed red and he weighed about seventy pounds. He was clumsy and too smart. The other kids hated him.

When I got off the bus at the mall stop, the girls got off behind me. I could hear them following, giggling behind their manicures.

Between the sets of double doors at the entrance, they surrounded me, Mackenzie and Taylor blocking my path and Morgan to my left. I felt like I was being taunted by a pack of vicious surnames.

"Come on," I said. "Let me in."

"Why?"

"I just need to buy some stuff, okay?"

"With what money, huh? You don't look like you have any money. Oh, unless your mama whored some for you. Or maybe she sold some extra drugs."

Fury bloomed in a spot at the nape of my neck and spread until I felt my face flushed with it. Who were these girls to talk about Mama or me like this? What did they know?

Taylor's eyes widened and looked suddenly startled and I realized I'd pushed her into the glass door. I watched her eyelids narrow to slits and felt her palms strong against my chest. And then I was falling, my hands flailing stupidly in empty air. I was so busy groping for a hold that I forgot to use my hands to break my fall. My head cracked against the tile floor.

"You stupid bitch." The words floated above me, disembodied.

I couldn't see which girl spoke. Bursting stars took up the whole of my vision. I don't know how long I lay there before I got up on my elbows to see that the girls had gone.

A small crowd of shoppers gathered and helped me to my feet. I swayed and an older man in a brown Stetson steadied me.

"Sorry," I said for no reason. "I'm okay."

They clucked at me for a minute or two until I insisted I was fine and then they were gone too.

I passed through the entrance. The heat and buzz inside the stores made my head swim and my stomach churn. I reeled into the washroom and got sick into a toilet. That was when I decided to catch the bus home empty-handed.

In the apartment, Granny examined the back of my scalp, parting my hair like a monkey searching for lice. I winced when she pushed around the bump on my head. I had told her what had happened, but left out the part where I got sick in the mall washroom.

"Looks all right to me. It didn't puncture the skin but you've got a goose egg, that's for sure. Go get undressed and I'll run you a bath."

I pulled my clothes off slowly, feeling sore all over, and was grateful for the steaming heat when my body went under the water.

I was sitting up in bed reading when Granny came in and sat on the side of my mattress.

"You're not well liked are you?" Granny asked.

If this was her way of comforting me, I wondered where she was going with it. I just stared at her and waited.

"I wasn't well liked either. Nor was your mother. But believe you me, bullies have a way of biting themselves in the arse. That girl who hit you will get hers someday."

I supposed that was some sort of comfort; I just couldn't figure out what sort.

"Granny, I'm sorry."

"What on earth do you have to be sorry for?"

"I was going out to buy you a Christmas present when those girls came around. Christmas Day is tomorrow and I didn't get a chance to get you anything."

"Let that be a lesson to you, then, about procrastination."

She got up and walked to the door. When she turned to me, her expression was a curious mix of emotions I hadn't seen on her before. She said, "I don't need anything for Christmas anyway. Good night."

My second encounter with my mother's boyfriend, Julian, came after Christmas, in the night. Voices woke me, suppressed giggles, shuffling feet. I lay still in my bed, listening to electric whispers over the sound of the surging blood in my head, which still pounded from my fall. I didn't know who it was, although I suspected it was Mama with her key, and someone else.

I watched the door to my room, but it stayed closed. I heard them go past.

Granny's voice suddenly rang out through the dark. "What are you doing here at this time of night?"

A man's voice mumbled words, low and indistinct.

"Get out," Granny said.

The other voice rose and deepened, urgent and clear. "We'll go when you give us what we came for. Cough it up."

"I don't know what you're talking about."

"I say you know exactly what I'm talking about."

"I'll call the police. I mean it."

"No you won't, bitch."

The sharp sound of a bell clanged as the telephone hit the other side of my bedroom wall and fell to the floor.

The noises that came afterward smelled like fear, like metal in my nostrils.

With a *thunk*, my bedroom door came open and in an instant Mama was beside my bed. Her breath blew sour against my dry, hot cheek.

"Shit, shit, shit. Annabel, take this and use it. Oh, God."

She placed a small weight on the covers over my chest and then was gone.

I heard some more knocking around before the silence came, strong like a vacuum in space, like nothing.

I couldn't move forever. I lay listening, expecting something, but unsure what, my eyes clamped closed. I might have slept.

A minute — or maybe hours — later, a beam of sunlight shot around my blind, searing a temporary mark onto the carpet of my room. Things seemed safer in the morning. I tested the movement of my limbs, which were no longer paralyzed.

I got up and stripped off my sweat-damp pyjamas. I pulled on a clean pair of grey jogging pants and a fleece shirt. The normalcy of these rituals made me believe I'd see Granny sitting on her bed fully clothed and ready to criticize my unladylike wardrobe.

I crept out my door and down toward her room. Her door hung open and through it I could see what had happened.

Granny lay across the bed in her white cotton nightgown, one leg on the bed, the other on the floor. It was a careless way to lie, and normally she would be mortified to be caught in such a pose.

One step closer. I saw a gash and a purple bruise, like the bloom of a blue morning glory, on her forehead. Beside the bed, her ceramic table lamp lay in a heap of jumbled shards.

There was no sound of breathing except my own ragged gasps. I felt like I was upright but everything in the room was upside down. All the dresser drawers were pulled out and dumped across the floor. The window blinds had been ripped down and lay on the carpet under the sill.

And then I remembered that Mama had placed something on top of me. I went back to my bedroom and found it on the floor, a little silver cell phone. Dialing 911 now wouldn't help Granny. It was too late. Too late to hear her grumbling voice, to feel her hand on my forearm while we walked along a winter slippery sidewalk, to tell her how I felt about everything she'd done for me.

I put the phone on my dresser and went back into Granny's room. I arranged her on the bed and pulled the covers over her. And then I got in too. I put her left arm straight out and lay down in the crook of it. I smoothed her greying hair away from her face and laid my head against her shoulder. Somehow, curling up in bed with her didn't seem strange at all, but comforting.

When I took her hand in mine, I noticed her fingernails were ragged from the struggle. I remembered how I had not been able to shout for help or move during what I now realized was unspeakable violence.

I lay in bed with my granny and slept and woke and slept for the rest of the day.

When I finally dialed 911, sometime on New Year's Eve, on the cell phone Mama had left for me, I discovered I couldn't say a word. I hung up and dialed again from the kitchen phone. I put the receiver on the counter and left the operator saying, "What is the nature of your emergency?" over and over again, while I went back to Granny and waited.

When I think about it, I spent a hell of a lot of my young life waiting. Waiting for Mama, for a normal life, for love, for an emergency response team.

I believe Granny wanted to love me as much as I wanted to love her. Maybe wanting to love each other was close enough to the real thing for us both.

Chapter 8

Jerome showed me a wooden box he had made.

"I made it out of cedar," he said. "It took me forty hours in the shed, I counted. Bobby taught me how."

The box was plain and oblong, about the size of one of Granny's English tea chests, with a design carved in the top: a bear on all fours with a fish in its mouth.

"I carved the bear myself. The lid doesn't fit exactly," Jerome said, poking at the wonky lid while I admired the whole contraption. "But I know what I did wrong. I'll do it right if I make another one. And I'll do it faster, too."

I swept my fingers over the smooth wood, lacquered thick and shiny. Beautiful.

He plucked it from my reluctant grasp.

"You want me to make one for you?"

I didn't shake my head no; I couldn't. I wanted one of those boxes.

"I'll make another one. I want to. I could use the practice. You can help me with it, if you like."

We started later the same day, out in the shed, with two weeks to go before the start of the school year. Jerome begged two short planks of cedar from Bobby and shooed him out so we could work on it without any help. Jerome measured the rectangular sides onto the wood and helped me use the jigsaw to cut it. The whirr and buzz, the control, the smell of cedar, helped me understand what Jerome loved about woodworking.

The last of the long summer days let us take our time and, bit-by-bit, we transformed the beauty of plain wood into a different kind of beauty. An object of function and utility as well as prettiness.

I sanded the edges of the lid until they were curved and smooth all around.

I found a picture of a rose in one of Mary's women's magazines. Mama loved roses. With a pencil, Jerome sketched an image of the flower onto a spare piece of wood, and then showed me how to use different sizes of chisels to etch it on. The tools were clumsy in my hands and I messed it up a few times before I felt confident enough to try it on the actual lid.

Ten days from when we started, my box was ready for its two thick coats of lacquer. The stuff stank worse than new markers and made my head spin, but when the lacquer dried, the grain of the wood shone through, pure as life. My rose darkened and looked more real.

I cut two perfect rectangles out of a piece of rich, purple velvet and hot-glued them onto the underside of the lid and the bottom of the box.

"You did good," said Jerome, and smiled with pride at our creation. "You can keep your jewelry in it."

I had never got my ears pierced and no one had ever given me anything made of gemstones or precious metal. I had no jewelry. Even if I did, I wouldn't have kept it in that box.

Mama had beautiful gold and diamond jewelry and I could picture her putting the pieces carefully in the box that her daughter made for her. I could see the smile of pride on her face. It warmed me through. The box I made was a secret gift for the one who was coming.

⌁⌁⌁

Late in the afternoon of the day I finished the box, the weather turned dark. Rain fell past my window in a metallic sheet that shone with dull silver light. It showered so thick and fast I couldn't make out individual droplets in the air. The roof drummed a rhythm. Rain like this made me humble, awed. The clean smell of wet earth came through the screen in damp gusts against my face.

I left my room and ran downstairs to the back door. Tully stood ready in his black rain boots and green slicker. I grabbed my larger green slicker that hung on a peg by the door, and put it on, along with my yellow rubber boots.

"I talked to Jerome," said Tully. "He'll meet us outside. Let's go."

We'd done this, the three of us, whenever it rained, since an afternoon early last summer, when we were caught out in the field by a surprise storm. It had blown into the sky in a matter of minutes and the downpour blasted us before we had a chance to head for the house. We started to make a run for it, but Tully had struggled in the newly churned mud and tall grasses. I grabbed Jerome's arm and we looked back. Already as wet as we could be, we waited for him.

Jerome looked into the sky and said, "Holy crap, this is cool. Try this. Look straight up and watch it come down on you."

I did, and so did Tully when he caught up.

"It's like Star Wars, when they go into warp speed, or whatever, and all the stars go blasting past the Millennium Falcon. It's just like that."

There we stood, wild and abandoned, water belting into our faces. We didn't care that we were soaking, our shoes squelching, filled with water, tepid from the warmth of our feet.

The storm died as suddenly as it had arisen and thin lemon sun lit Jerome and Tully's faces through a haze of sizzling mist.

The boys laughed and whooped with joy, and we ran the rest of the way to the house, smiling and dripping.

Now, Tully and I walked to the middle of the yard and looked into the sky. The rain fell so heavily I was instantly soaked through. My hood slipped off when I tipped my head back but I didn't bother to pull it up.

I saw the individual droplets now, some whizzing past my head and some splotching fat and wet on my cheeks and chin. I blinked away the ones that found my eyeballs.

Jerome came out and stood on the other side of me.

Tully's hand felt for mine and gripped it. I reached out for Jerome's hand, so anyone watching from the house wouldn't think it meant anything that I held hands with only Tully, whose palm felt warm and slippery in my cold fingers. I tightened my grip and he tightened his.

We had once invited Char to join us in the rain but she refused, not interested in getting wet and mucky. I forgot to wonder where Graydon was, or whether he might like to come out with us.

This was *our* feeling. This wonderment.

❧❧❧

Bored and lazy on a summer morning, Jerome, Tully, Graydon and I lay behind the house in the shadow of an overgrown maple tree playing a loose game of Truth or Dare. We didn't let Char play anymore. With her, there was a little too much truth and way too much dare. I didn't play either; I just listened to the boys talk and challenge one another to do stupid things.

It was Tully's turn to ask Jerome.

"Truth or dare?"

"Truth, I guess," said Jerome.

"What are you most scared of?"

Jerome looked at the back of his dark hand, brought a finger to his lips and bit off a piece of nail. He spat it into the grass and turned his face to the sky.

"Well, it used to be spiders. Isn't that freaking stupid? Scared of a little damn bug? Around here, spiders aren't even poisonous. I don't get how you can be scared of shit that don't kill you."

"He didn't ask what you *aren't* scared of, dick-wad," said Graydon.

"Nuts," Jerome said. We thought he was swearing again, so we waited for him to continue. He smiled.

"I'm allergic to peanuts. And you're the dick-wad, just so you know. If I eat a nut, my goddamn throat closes and I turn blue and die. It happened to me a couple of times before. Not the dying part." He laughed. "Imagine if you plugged your nose and sucked air through a straw. Now someone seals the end of the straw with their thumb. That's what it feels like."

Thinking about it made me take a deep breath of summer sweet air.

Jerome shook his head and stretched out across the lawn, lacing his fingers together over his belly. We all stared at him in silence, only a cicada hum on the air.

Jerome squinted at Graydon. "Truth or Dare, Stretch?"

Graydon jiggled his leg with nervous motion. He always seemed about to spring to his feet and run off somewhere.

"Dare," he said.

Jerome pushed up off the grass and crossed his legs lotus-style. "You sure, Asshole?"

"I'm sure, Shit-for-Brains."

"You know that new horse, arrived last week? You have to sneak out after dark and ride him. You gotta stay on for two minutes. And we all have to see you do it."

My head was shaking no before Jerome had finished talking. Graydon looked at me from between strands of his hair and I grabbed his wrist, placing an emphatic no behind my eyes.

"Yeah, okay," he said, still looking right into my face.

"That's crazy." Tully got up and brushed grass from his knees. "That horse'll kill you, and Mary'll eat you on toast for breakfast."

"I'll tell you what's crazy, Midget Boy. Owning a bunch of horses, paying to keep them, and not even riding them. That's fucking crazy."

"Midnight, then, right?" said Jerome. "We'll meet at the main gate."

"I'm not coming," said Tully. "I don't want to sit around and watch you kill yourself."

"Really? And here I thought that's exactly what you wanted." Graydon looked at me and winked. I felt a sick sensation rise from the bottom of my stomach.

The horse was Warrior, a huge dapple-grey stallion that Mary had said came from a ranch where he'd been beaten and starved for not doing whatever they'd wanted him to do. When I had tried to feed him that morning, he was still wild with fear and uncertainty and wouldn't come into the paddock. New horses had to live away from the rest of the herd at first, so Bobby had fenced a separate area for them to get used to the farm, the smells, sights and sounds. "Horses are sensitive creatures," he said. I took Warrior's breakfast to him there, but he still wouldn't eat. Mary said, "Trust takes time."

If those stupid boys tried to ride that crazy horse, they might ruin him for good, kill themselves, or both. But I didn't know what to do.

Everybody got up and started moving in separate directions. I tried to appeal to Jerome, pulling on his arm and shaking my head, angry that he even suggested Graydon do this dangerous stunt. Was he trying to kill him?

"Get off me, Ghost. It's all been agreed on and that's that. Give it up." He shrugged me off and went toward Bobby's shed.

"They won't listen to you." Tully squinted up at me through his glasses, a mirror to the blue sky. "It's all that macho junk. A dare's a dare."

That's that. A dare's a dare. It all sounded so foolish I wanted to scream at them, but they'd probably ignore me or call me a silly girl.

I fretted away the afternoon. The idea of writing a note to tell Mary (even anonymously) came and went. Not telling Mary amounted to a betrayal of her, but I was a foster kid and they were foster kids. We had to be in this together or I could kiss their companionship goodbye, for good. I'd be shunned and I was lonely enough already without losing Jerome. Or Graydon. All I wanted was for him to love me back.

I didn't worry about Tully. It would take more than a petty broken confidence for Tully to turn his back on me. He was against Graydon doing the dare anyway, not that he'd tell Mary either. Nobody would tell Mary.

Later that day Char figured out something was up and went after Graydon. He let her in on the secret and her eyes took on a sparkly glow. I think she was pretending the challenge had something to do with her. Like she was a fairy princess and

Graydon and Jerome were going to duel for her hand. She had a lot of romantic ideals for a girl in her situation.

I sat anxious on the fence rail, watching Warrior charge around from corner to corner. I thought and thought, but aside from begging — which I'd already tried — I couldn't come up with a way to stop it. Warrior probably sensed how uneasy I felt and it made him nervous.

Chapter 9

Dark seeped out of creeping shadows to give everything a sinister bluish purple hue.

The temperature of the warm summer day had dropped at dusk and now a kind of fog rose from the horses, black rocks, fence posts, and from us as we stood like stones in a graveyard. Anticipation fluttered in every breath. I was restless with the fear that Mary would sense our misdeeds on the breeze, that from her bed she would hear the pounding of my heart.

I stood at the rail, as close to Warrior as he'd let me, and hummed to calm him, or myself. Steam rose off the animal's great back and clouded from his pink-veined nostrils, which flared with anxiety.

Graydon paced along the straw-strewn concrete and pulled at his thumbnail with his teeth. Char leaned against the side of the barn and twirled a piece of her hair around her index finger.

"Hurry it up, man." Jerome made a get-a-move-on motion from his seat on a hay bale, his booted feet crossed at the ankles.

"How the hell am I supposed to get on him? He doesn't stand still for a second." Graydon's voice was strained through a veil of worry. He sounded like Granny used to when she knew Mama was coming for a visit.

"Your problem."

Graydon hadn't even gone into the paddock yet. He paced outside it watching Warrior, whose muscular neck shone with sweat in the flat glow of the farm's night-lights. Our breathing built a rhythm with the whap-whap of suicidal moths that threw their pale bodies against the barn light.

"Fuck it."

In one motion, Graydon leapt over the fence rail and into the ring with Warrior. The horse reared in magnificent panic, his hooves flailing through the night, backing into a corner in the process.

Graydon crouched, wrapping his skinny arms protectively around his head. He edged closer to Warrior, who was back on all fours and now produced a low grunting sound with every shallow breath.

I gripped the rail with my hands to slow their shaking and the rest of my body took up the tremble.

It all happened in an instant that seemed like hours. Warrior skirted Graydon in a sweep that made me flinch. Graydon dropped to his knees. Warrior thundered toward the opposite fence and I thought for an instant that he might charge straight through it. Instead, he flew. His front hooves left the earth, the muscles of his back legs straining with his full weight, and then he appeared to hang in midair. I leaned forward, held my breath and didn't let it out until all four of Warrior's hooves hit the earth on the other side of the paddock fence. He bolted off into the main field, his grey rump disappearing, swallowed by mist and gloom.

I raised a fist and whooped after his freedom, despite myself.

"Holy shit," said Jerome, who had left his hay bale to stand beside me at the fence. "Did you see that? That was worth the goddamn price of admission."

"I'm okay, by the way." Graydon had walked back over, slapping dirt from the knees of his jeans. "Thanks for asking."

"What a great relief," Jerome said. "You need to change into a new pair of boxers or what?"

"Very funny." Graydon stooped under the top rail and came out to stand with the rest of us.

"I think you were super brave." Char grasped him around the neck and I looked at the ground. Out of the corner of one eye I saw Graydon take her wrists and pull her arms to her sides.

"Thanks," he said.

And I looked up to see him staring at me.

Graydon spent the month of August being sweet. He didn't try to get into my shorts. Strange, I both wanted sex with him and didn't, but I took his lead and remained content with warm kisses on cool nights, and some heavy petting. The bottom half of his desires were being satisfied by Char. Not that I'd ever seen them together after that first time, but you don't have to see a thing to know that it's true. I remembered how he'd pulled Char's arms off his neck, right in front of me.

Any jealousy I started out with evaporated in the heat of Graydon's attention. I knew the truth about him and Char by the way she acted when he was around. Arrogant and superior, like she knew something the rest of us didn't. She was only working at fooling herself, though, because everybody knew they were doing it (except Mary and Bobby, who would've hit the roof). And, as far as I could tell, nobody much cared, me included. It was common knowledge that if you had the top half of a boy, you had the boy. The bottom half was nothing but instinct, only a primitive creature, much like Char herself, if you asked me.

Mary wondered aloud what had spooked Warrior into jumping out of the paddock that night, but it all faded away because by late morning it was clear that Warrior had made a friend: Nacho, of all creatures. I saw them out there, Nacho standing straight-legged right under Warrior's great frame, not even tall enough to touch the underside of his belly.

The summer finally wore itself out and the wind sent rumours that fall was coming. Bobby took us into the city to get our new school supplies. Reflected in the others' faces, I saw my own anticipation mixed with apprehension. Beginning a school year was like making a New Year's resolution that we weren't likely to keep. *This year I'll study hard, get straight A's, make Mary proud.*

In the office supply store, Graydon pushed a red plastic cart with a wonky wheel, his features set in a thoughtful expression. And I felt certain he wasn't thinking about how annoying the cart was, the way it kept veering to the right instead of going straight. I hoped he thought about me, but whatever he thought, it belonged to him alone. Jerome kept pushing Tully out of his way while Tully tried unsuccessfully to stand his ground. Char dropped a single pack of pencils into the cart and then sat yawning on a bench beside the front door, picking at the dry skin on her elbows.

We trudged through the aisles consulting our lists and pulling stuff into the cart: geometry sets, packages of lined paper, calculators, binders, pencils and pens.

On a shelf at the back I spotted the most wonderful dictionary I had ever seen. The pages were onionskin thin and crammed with tiny type. It must have had every word anyone had ever uttered in all the history of the English language, and was thousands of pages thick and bound in brown leather. I touched it. I hefted it up in both hands, opened it and scanned the pages, hungry to read all the words, new and old.

"Ghost, come on already," said Jerome. "We're done."

I put the dictionary back and joined the boys in the checkout queue.

By the time we shuffled into the farmhouse, rustling plastic bags and dragging tired feet, Mary had cooked a meal of spaghetti and meatballs, and had baked a chocolate cake. The house smelled like a home where a real family lived, cozy with Mary and warm food.

High school was scheduled to start right after Labour Day weekend and everyone had ants in their pants. None of us had ever fit in well at school, but Tully had had the worst time. His dwarfism was like a bull's eye on his back. Far from being overlooked because of his smallness, he stood out like a giant.

I looked pretty ordinary, except I kept my hair short when all the girls wore it long, and I dressed in baggy boy's clothes, hiding my girl-ness behind a boy veneer. When other students teased me about my looks and my silence, I would stand still as a statue and look at my shoes. They mostly eased off and eventually quit. You could poke at a statue all day long, but it'll never move or talk back.

I felt as antsy as anyone else around the farm, but not only about school. Mama was supposed to get out of the drug rehab centre in early September. She had promised to call me right when she got out, and I was as jittery about getting the call as I was about the prospect of not getting it.

I knew she'd been scared sober by what had happened to us, and going into detox and then rehab had been her only option.

A sober Mama would make all the right decisions. I knew it. It was the drugs that had screwed everything up for both of us.

Added to nightmares about Mama, the thought of going back to high school to begin a whole new year chilled me through. I didn't have many happy memories of school.

The public school I went to when I was eleven had been long, low and made of red brick. Architecturally speaking, it was nothing but a box to learn in.

Toward the front of the building, a curious and unexplained (to us, anyway) brick hole went up the side. It was probably some kind of leftover chimney that didn't get used anymore. It began something like four feet off the ground and inside was about two feet by two feet wide.

Every day at recess the kids tortured Patrick Rantin, who was the only boy who ever talked to me. He was actually bright and funny, and would help me with my math homework when I was struggling with concepts like multiplying fractions.

One day, when the bullies were happily spitting on him and pulling his shirt over his head, an especially large boy had a bright idea.

"Come here, Rantin. I have something to show you."

Patrick shook his pale red head. "I don't wanna."

Another kid shoved him from behind and he was forced to take a step toward the larger boy, who grabbed him and kicked him roughly until he'd forced him under the brick hole. His head smacked against it when he was going under and I heard him cry out.

"Get up in there, you stupid dick-head."

"Don't make me." His whimper took on a hint of fear. The boy started hoofing at Patrick's white legs, which was all any of us could see of him now. Slowly, the legs disappeared up the hole. For the entire recess, the boys took turns guarding the hole so Patrick couldn't get out. We heard his frantic squeals, panicky and scared.

I waited close by, not knowing what to do. No one else cared anything about Patrick. They all gawked and then walked away when they got bored with the show.

The bell signalled the end of recess and the yard emptied. I watched Patrick's stick legs unfold and touch the ground and then he ducked and emerged from the hole. His bright purple face was streaked with dirt, tears and snot.

"What are you lookin' at?" he asked me.

"You okay?"

"Yeah. Shit. No." He dropped to the grass, hugged his bruised knees and cried. I sat beside him, waiting until he was done.

"You want to tell the office? I'll go with you, if you want to tell," I said.

"No. I just wanna go home."

I walked Patrick the few blocks to his house and then I went to the park and hung around, swinging on the swings, taking a slide or two. If I went back to school they'd want to know where I'd been. If I went home, Granny would give me the third degree. I had to do what Patrick wanted and keep it on the down low. When it got late enough, I went home.

Patrick was back at school the next day. I never saw them shove him into the hole again, but the abuse went on for the rest of the year. I don't know how he stood it. I preferred to be ignored. I bet he wished he could have been ignored too.

We stayed friends up into high school and I wondered what he was doing now? I figure there's a guy like Patrick Rantin in every school the world over, the perfect victim who won't fight back, won't tell. At any moment it could happen to Jerome or Char, Tully or me.

I hoped not to witness bullying like that during my grade ten year. That kind of violence made me sick to my stomach. I had seen the path where real violence could take you. Then I was struck by a realization. I knew one thing for sure: bullying wouldn't happen to a guy like Graydon.

⟶⟶⟶

Labour Day weekend ended and we were all swallowed by a yellow bus and carted off to school. In the morning I'd shoved Graydon's plastic lighter into the pocket of my pants. If I couldn't be near him, I wanted to have something of his close to me, to give me strength.

Char had just about chewed her fingers off during the week before school started, and she sat on the green vinyl bus seat with a face like thunder.

I was pretty sure she lived in fear that someone would discover she didn't know how to read. I figured most people knew but thought she was a lost cause, nothing but a street hooker without a future. She'd spent only half of last year in school, the other half she spent hooking full time before she got arrested and sent to live with Mary and Bobby. Her teachers gave her all Ds, she told us, and passed her to the next grade anyway. Even though I could barely stand the sight of her, I felt sorry for Char because nobody cared.

⟶⟶⟶

People had been gentle with me at first, after they discovered me in bed with Granny that New Year's Eve. The police asked me questions but didn't press me too hard for answers.

In interrogation rooms, I memorized my feet. The laces of the cross trainers I wore wove X's across the tongue. In the low light, I noticed the highly reflective properties of the checkmark-shaped patches on the sides, traced them with my fingers.

After a week, the pressure on me grew. The police had to know what happened so they could put my mother's boyfriend away forever. Did I want the same thing to happen to someone else? I didn't. I made an effort to tell them what I remembered about that night. I could hear the sounds of the struggle in my nightmares; smell my own fear when I heard his voice through my wall. But I had no words for any of it, not the ideas or the objects. I looked at a telephone, knew what it was and what it was used for, but if the word existed for me at all, it was permanently behind a wall in my brain. Even the word for murder sat stuck behind that wall.

I tried to write everything down, but found my hand paralyzed with terror. Writing it down meant reliving it, and I couldn't do that. Officer Davies took the blank piece of paper and I watched her face while she stared at it. Officer Davies was young and pretty, with blond hair that she pulled back into a little bun right in the centre of the back of her head. I wanted to be her so badly.

"Sweetie," she said. "We need your help. If you can't talk to us, you have to at least write it down. You have to try."

I'd already tried, but I tried again. Speaking was physically impossible and when I tried to write it down, I got sweaty and my heart raced until I thought it might burst. I concluded right then that the best way for me to survive was not to communicate at all.

In the end they had enough evidence without my written statement. Mama picked Julian out of a lineup and, when she sobered up, she talked and talked, enough for both of us. I later saw the inch-thick report on Officer Davies' desk.

They said the motive was robbery, and that was why Julian ransacked Granny's bedroom.

"Were they looking for money?" Officer Davies asked me.

I shrugged. The rumour of money had always hovered over me and Granny but that was only Mama's delusion. Surely, if there were money, Granny would've spent some of it to make our lives more comfortable. Nothing in that apartment was worth anything. There had been nothing to steal, and yet he'd killed my granny.

The last time I saw Mama was before she went off to jail. We sat on either side of a stainless steel table. Mama smoked and looked tired.

"I'm sorry, Annabel," she said. "Look what I've done to you."

I wanted her to pull me into a hug and never let me go, but she didn't touch me.

"I've made some big mistakes. When I get out, things are going to be different. We'll get a place together, you and me, no men this time. I'm through with men."

Mama's promise was what kept me going, through teary one-sided sessions with Dr. Schmidtlein, more interviews with Officer Davies, one foster family and then another, until I found Noble Spirit, and Mary and Bobby.

Now, on the bus, the thought of Mama's promised phone call obsessed me. I couldn't concentrate on anything. I felt a balloon of excitement expand under my diaphragm.

I didn't even care when a boy in my chemistry class stuck his finger in his throat and made gagging noises in the direction of his buddies when I walked past him to my seat.

My mama was coming to take me away, to start again, together.

I had found a red ribbon in Mary's sewing kit and had tied it around my wooden box. It was as ready for Mama as I was.

By the end of the first week of school, I was positively dying of anticipation; my fingernails as bitten to the nub as Char's had been on the first day. The weekend felt like a torment, every second an interminable physical tick forward.

On Tuesday morning, Mary's alarm clock failed and we missed the bus by more than an hour.

"Jeez, let's go people!" shouted Tully, standing by the door. "Come on." He hated to be late.

Bobby had to get his shoes on and drive us to school in the truck, on his way to work at the Catholic high school. Mary had the small kitchen TV on while she puttered, and the breakfast television show she was watching cut abruptly to a breaking news report.

None of us was much interested in news, so we would have passed it by if Mary hadn't squeaked and cupped both hands over her mouth.

"What is it?" asked Bobby.

"Oh my God, Bobby."

We moved, shoes and all, to crowd around the countertop TV, jostling to see the screen. A tall city building smoked like a newly extinguished birthday candle.

"An airplane," said Mary. "An airplane flew right into that building. I saw it happen."

"Let's go to the living room," said Graydon. "Where we can see it better."

On the bigger television, the scene looked twice as frightening. It seemed like the whole world was on fire and waiting for what would happen next. Another airplane circled and crashed into another tower. There were people in those planes, people in those buildings.

When the first tower crumbled, we gasped at the great plumes of brown dust, the screams of bystanders. A man jumped from certain death to even more certain death. And then a woman jumped too.

Tully sat beside me on the couch, his red ball cap crushed in one hand.

I wondered where my mama was right at that moment. This tragedy, this terrible nightmare, was happening in New York, but what proof did I have that she wasn't in one of those buildings, or on one of those airplanes? Until last week, she was safe and sound, first in a jail cell, and most recently in a cozy room at the rehab centre. Now, she could be anywhere.

I wondered if Mama worried about me the way I worried about her. If this horror started World War III, I might never see Mama again. Disaster scenes ran through my head, mothers screaming in terror for their babies. Children wide-mouthed and howling for their mamas.

As panic took hold of me, threatening to turn me inside out, I felt Tully's small hand in mine. I looked over at him. His cheeks and eyelashes behind his glasses were shining with tears. I gripped his hand and felt Mary, who sat beside Tully, reach around and press both of us into her bosom. I didn't feel exactly safe, but at least we all had one another.

We didn't go to school that day. We watched as much of the news coverage as we could bear, and then went our own ways, to our own comforts and reassurances. I spent two hours grooming Jett, and then Twilight and Nacho. I noticed that the cut on Nacho's rump had healed well.

That evening after supper we crowded into the living room to watch more news coverage. My head was still twisted with worry that the world might end and then the phone jingled through the rooms of the farmhouse. The phone didn't ring much, and whenever it did, everyone stopped and waited until the person nearest the receiver picked it up. This time, Mary, who was standing by the door, went to the kitchen and answered it. She talked for a short time, but I couldn't hear what she said. I was afraid to move. She came into the living room. My heart flipped once in my chest.

"Ghost, honey, it's your mama." She held the receiver out to me. For a moment I forgot how to move my body.

I recovered and put the phone to my ear.

"Hi, Annabel, Sweetheart!" Mama sounded cheery. I was sure that wasn't a good thing.

"Mary tells me you still aren't talking. I wish you were. I'd love to hear your voice." Mama sounded sober and I allowed myself a moment of hope. "She says you're doing well there at the farm. I never would have thought of you as a farm girl, but Mary says you've got a real thing going for the horses."

She paused and the silence ate me up.

"I wanted to check up on you. Let you know I'm still alive." She laughed, a weird, hollow sound. "That's some crazy stuff happening in New York, huh? Listen, I don't want you to be too disappointed, but I think it's better if you stay with Mary, at least for a little bit longer. I have a good lead on a job, but it's out in Vancouver. I can't afford to take you with me yet, but I'll send for you when I can. We'll be together soon, don't you worry."

Mama said another few nothings, and when I hung up, I didn't feel anything one way or another, which surprised me. I sat back down and picked up my book. The only thing was, I couldn't read it.

"You okay, honey?" asked Mary.

I met her gaze and nodded. She put her hand on my shoulder. I saw it there but it felt weightless and transparent, a shadow hand.

Mama would not be coming for me. The world could end and I'd be ready. An airplane could smash right into the window of my bedroom and I wouldn't care. I was willing to bet I'd never see Mama again either way.

I got off the couch and went to bed.

Chapter 10

Each day the school bus rattled me along to where the teachers sang their vacant teaching songs. After school, the horses in the paddock sniffed at my empty pockets. In the kitchen Mary made food I didn't want to eat, and people everywhere spoke words I didn't try to understand.

Everything moved along the same as always, but somehow nothing was the same. The world that had once been filled with the vibrant colours, sounds and scents of living plants and animals had become a drab nothingness. To get out of bed required an effort that I didn't believe I had until I found my feet on the floor, propelling me forward through one more hour of one more day.

I took the wooden box out of my dresser drawer and stared at it. I'd been impatient, should have practiced more. The design I had carved looked like random curves instead of the beautiful rose I had wanted it to be. The glue had dried in globs under the bits of velvet. The box looked amateurish.

I threw it in my wastebasket, ribbon and all.

At school, the eyes of the other kids looked haunted, like Patrick Rantin's that day the bullies shoved him up the hole. I felt like I was walking around in a prison full of dead eyes.

In the evenings I went to bed early but didn't sleep.

One Sunday in the paddock, Graydon tried to lure me into his kisses, but I resisted, feeling hard like a piece of twisted driftwood.

The sun shone with such Indian summer warmth that I wore only a T-shirt and a pair of jeans, plastic water sandals on my feet. It wasn't the best choice around heavy and sharp-hoofed horses, but I didn't care.

"Come on. Snap out of it, Ghost," Graydon said, his smooth, summer-darkened hand on my forearm. I shrugged him off and he went away.

I walked out of the paddock and into the barn to get the currycomb to use on Jett, but the grooming bucket I kept it in wasn't hanging from its usual nail. People were so careless. I always found buckets, halters and bits of grooming equipment scattered around on the ground. Why couldn't people put things where they belonged?

I wandered toward Bobby's work shed, scanning the ground. I didn't find any brushes, but around the side of the shed, against the wall, someone had propped four panes of glass all in a row, blue with sky reflection, smooth and perfect. Not a smudge marred their surfaces; they were like pools of undisturbed water.

I stepped right up close to one, but it reflected only the sky. I didn't have a reflection at all. I didn't exist. I had become a real ghost.

The songs of birds and insects stopped. The breeze died. Clean outdoor scents rushed away and all that remained was a metallic taste on my tongue and in my nostrils.

I backed up, dodging slightly, trying to get the glass to catch my reflection. I stumbled over a rock, but caught my balance before I hit the ground. The rock I had tripped on was an ugly chunk of grey matter the size of a brain, the contours and pits in its surface holding fearful shadows.

I picked it up, the weight solid and real, and heaved it into the middle of one of the panes of glass. The glass shattered, collapsing upon itself, imploding, disappearing, irrelevant.

Another rock lay to my right, smaller than the first. I tossed that one into the second pane of glass. And again, until each of the four panes lay in shining bits across the packed earth along the side of the shed. I felt neither joy nor horror at the sight of what I had done, only a fuzzy blankness. Empty.

"Jesus Christ, Ghost, what did you do?" Jerome grabbed at my arm. "What the hell did you do?"

What had I done?

"Your hands. Your feet."

I looked down and saw blood oozing from slashes in my hands and on my sandaled feet. I didn't know how I had cut myself. Had I touched the broken glass? It didn't hurt.

Jerome pulled me around the shed and toward the house. I saw Mary running to us, swaying from side to side, the way Jett moved. It didn't seem to get her forward any faster than simply walking would have.

"Oh, Ghost," said Mary, out of breath. "What happened? Come on into the house and let's see what's what."

She went up the porch steps and held the screen door open for Jerome and me.

"She broke all the new windows for the shed. Every one." Jerome didn't sound angry; he sounded awestruck, verging on frightened.

"Jerome, get me some clean towels from the linen closet."

Mary sat me on the kitchen counter as if I were a small child and bathed my hands and feet in the sink. I watched my blood rise into the swirling water where it became clouds of rust and disappeared.

"It doesn't look so bad now," said Mary, as much to reassure herself, it seemed, as me. "Only a few small cuts. Some Band-Aids should do the trick."

Mary moved me to a kitchen chair, fresh towels wrapped around my hands and feet, and rummaged in the cupboards for a package of bandages. By now, Jerome had told everyone within earshot what I'd done.

Char's thin face hovered in my vision, her gaze neither worried nor caring, only curious.

"Are you crazy?" she asked.

"She's not crazy," said Tully stretching himself as tall as he could and managing to reach the level of Char's belt buckle. "She's just upset."

"I'm sure if you all thought real hard," said Mary. "You'd think of some homework you could be doing."

At the mention of homework, there were mumbles of feeding horses, stacking wood and other outdoor chores that suddenly needed attending to. Jerome, Tully and Char drifted away and out the door.

The house was almost empty. I saw Graydon sitting at a distance in one of the kitchen chairs, watching me, his expression blank, unreadable. An elbow on each knee, his fingers intertwined below his chin. I hadn't realized he was there.

Now that Mary had cleaned and dressed my cuts, they began to smart. She took my chin in her hand. I looked into her eyes and saw disappointment and mistrust. I had shattered more than glass.

"Go and lie down for a bit," she said.

I got up and walked on my heels, slowly, up the stairs to my room.

I lay on my bed and felt the biting sting of each gash. It felt good, better than numb nothingness.

❧❧❧

Hours later, the door to my room squeaked open and Bobby pushed his way through. He took an extra moment to fan the door back and forth a few times, looking into the near distance and listening to the hinges complaining, probably making a mental note to oil them.

I tensed, certain he'd be angry about what I had done. He had never come into my room.

He sat at the end of the bed and I pulled myself upright, dragging my feet — bare except for the several pinkish bandages — away from him. I bent my knees up into a tent and hugged them, resting my chin on the back of one hand.

His sandy hair stuck up wild, like an overused toothbrush. His face had pale stubble growing in patches around his chin and cheeks. He brought with him a smell of freshly sawn wood. He studied the pattern of my bedspread, running his hand over and over it. I listened to the tick-tick-tick of the threads as they caught the roughness of his palm.

Bobby sighed. "Ghost, there are things you don't understand about this situation. I can't say for sure if your mother actually wanted you to go to Vancouver with her. Yes, we know about the Vancouver plan. Her parole officer talked to your caseworker who talked to us. Either way, your mother isn't allowed to simply come here and take you. Someone should've explained all that. Mary and me are sorry you didn't understand. Your mother still has to apply to the courts to get custody returned to her. As far as I know, she hasn't done that.

"Her loss is our gain. Mary and me didn't want to let you go. We believe staying here is best for everyone. At least for now."

The crow's feet around his eyes crinkled in the late afternoon light that filtered through the dirt on the outside of my window. Bobby rocked forward, slapped his palms on his thighs, and got up off the bed. He pulled my door back and forth another few times.

"Supper's in five. Someone'll shout up for you when it's ready," he said and headed toward the stairs.

He hadn't mentioned the cuts on my hands and feet or the glass by the shed. He hadn't even asked me to pay for busting up his new windows.

By the next day all the fractured bits had disappeared from the ground. My cuts healed quickly but for weeks people treated me like the glass I had broken, as if I had *Fragile* tattooed on my forehead and I would break into pieces if I got shaken around too much.

Tully took to patting me softly on the arm, shoulder or thigh whenever he was nearby. Jerome seemed afraid of me, kind enough, but distant. Char ignored me.

But Graydon's reaction puzzled me most; he began to watch me. Instead of coming up and talking, or inviting me to the woods or into the barn to kiss, I frequently caught sight of him at a distance, neither moving toward me nor away, just staring. When I caught his gaze, he didn't look embarrassed and turn away, or smile and come up to me. He kept on looking.

It was mid-October before normal returned. The last of the curling leaves quivered on the trees, waiting for a strong wind to push them into a suicidal leap to their final resting place among their brown brothers and sisters, already waiting on the ground for burial by snow.

After some weeks, people put my crazy act behind them and relaxed around me. Tully put sleeping in my bed back into his nighttime rotation. I felt him touch my face when he thought I was asleep. Jerome returned to insulting me daily. Char flipped her hair in my direction, which was a step up from refusing to acknowledge my existence.

On a Saturday evening, while I lay reading in bed, Graydon squeezed through my bedroom door. He leaned his upper back against my wall, hands shoved in his pockets, very cool, and looked at me through bits of hair that straggled in front of his eyes.

I looked at his skinny body; it was wiry and strong, a deceptively simple machine, like a lever or a pulley, that had more strength than I could imagine.

"Meet me in the stable at midnight," he said. "I want to show you something."

I nodded.

After Graydon was gone, I fell to speculating wildly about what he might want to show me. I got as far as an engagement ring with a proposal before I told myself to smarten up and quit dwelling on fantasies. I would know by the witching hour.

I brushed my hair and sneaked into Char's empty room to grab a container of strawberry scented lip gloss. Char had special permission to spend the night at a schoolmate's house. All day she'd been annoyingly giddy about the prospect.

I dabbed the lip gloss on carefully, using the mirror in my room. I opened my window for a moment or two and let the frosty air clear the room of the overwhelming stink of artificial strawberry.

Romantic relationships among us kids were strictly verboten. In bed by eleven o'clock, no exceptions. Tully wasn't allowed to play musical beds either, but we kept that secret among ourselves. Mary frequently stated that it was her personal responsibility to make sure no hanky-panky went on behind her back, so we took up the challenge. And that was how we saw it too: a challenge. We loved and respected Mary, but people had told us what to do for our whole lives. Now we wanted to make our own decisions. We'd all grown up into big, adult-like people, except for Tully, and we felt strong. Getting pressed under authority's thumb got pretty tiresome and we did whatever we could to squeeze up out from underneath.

Whatever we did, the main thing was that we didn't want to get caught. Eluding capture was part of the appeal, for me anyway, and whatever Graydon wanted to show me in the barn after curfew definitely did not amount to anything innocent.

The time finally ticked over to five to twelve. The house creaked and settled into silence. I wanted to go out the window, like Juliet (did Juliet ever actually go out the window?), but my room was on the second floor and no handy trellis led safely to the ground.

I used the door instead, and crept downstairs to the hall. I grabbed my jacket, slid on my shoes, and went through the kitchen and out into a night sharp with cool starlight.

Pulling the jacket around me, I trudged through clouds of my own breath toward the stable, crushing tracks of frozen mud beneath my feet.

After I went through the stable door, I walked all the way down the row of stalls to the largest one at the end. Graydon sat on a mound of hay, his feet resting on a patch of bare concrete floor. A large coffee can sat between his feet, a small flame struggling above the top of the can, providing heat and light to the small space. He fed the flames with bits of wood and newspaper that he dropped into the can one by one. He didn't notice me until I was close enough to reach out and touch him. When he looked up it was as if he were waking from a dream.

I looked at the can and back at Graydon, worried about having a fire so close to all that hay and dry barn wood. But, if Graydon recognized what my look meant, he ignored it.

A small battery-powered camp lantern on one of the bales squeezed out a feeble yellow glow. He had spread a fleece blanket across two hay bales and I sat on it beside him. He picked up a bottle of Captain Morgan white rum, splashed some into a plastic cup from Mary's kitchen and handed it to me.

"I need you to drink with me," he said.

I had never drunk with anyone, but I took the cup and cradled it. He had drunk some already. I could see it in the softness around his eyes and the spots of pink high on his cheeks.

I wondered where he got it. Mary and Bobby were strict about alcohol. They didn't drink and didn't keep liquor in the house. I'd heard a rumour that Bobby had once been an alcoholic and didn't want temptation anywhere close by.

"I have my sources," he said.

He winked, clacked his plastic cup against mine, and took a quick shot. I downed mine too, and felt a roaring in my throat, stomach and then head. After a second or two, the roar settled to a buzz and the rum smoothed through me. Softening me. I was butter on a warm counter. I pulled off my jacket.

He was quiet for a time, and I hoped that a bottle of rum wasn't the only thing he wanted to show me. He took the drink from my hand and set it on the floor beside his. He pushed the flaming coffee can away from us with the toe of his boot.

"Life is shit, Ghost, you know that?" he said, his S's now blurred by rum. I knew that. "It's like a war zone. Like a series of battles you gotta fight if you want to survive. But the worst part is that you never know who to trust. Anyone can be a spy, out to get you. Strangers, friends, even family."

I knew what he meant.

"I haven't shown anybody this, but I want you to see, so you can understand me." He curled his hand around the back of my neck and brought his forehead close to mine. "I trust you."

He stood up and began undoing his belt buckle. I put my hand up to stop him.

"It's okay. You have to trust me too." He hesitated until I nodded, and then he put my hand back in my lap and returned to pulling down his fly. He turned his back to me, looking at my face over his shoulder, and pushed his pants and boxers down to his knees.

I stared at his buttocks, not able to believe what I saw. How had I not noticed this when his butt first waggled before my eyes, with Char's skinny body beneath it? The pale-orange light of the fire and the lemon glow of the lantern combined to be not quite enough. I leaned forward for a closer look. His ass was covered in round, white scars.

"Cigarettes. My old man put them where they'd hurt the most, and where no one could see them."

His father had done that to him.

He turned slowly to face me and moved his hands away from his genitals. They too, were pockmarked with blistered scars. I could hardly imagine the pain.

Graydon leaned toward me and took the hand that had gone to my mouth. He touched my forefinger to my cheek, moved my hand toward his crotch, and ran the wetness of my tear over one of the marks on his groin. The skin felt warm and as smooth as marble.

His penis, studded with old wounds, wobbled under my touch.

Graydon took a step toward me and I felt his palm against the back of my head.

"Kiss it better." I didn't know what he meant, what he wanted me to do, and then I did. And left Char's strawberry lip-gloss behind.

I lay back in the hay and he knelt over me, pulling off my clothing and his. I ran my hands over the hard muscles of his abdomen and across the strength of his slim back.

And then I followed him willingly, to the places I'd only ever been dragged to by Morrow in the darkness of my childhood bed. I wondered if Graydon considered me a virgin. I hoped so.

He tasted like sweet rum and his hands moved me this way and that, gentle across a dark blue blanket studded with stars, or maybe they were snowflakes. Bits of hay stuck into my shoulders and the backs of my legs through the blanket but I let Graydon position me until he had my pants down and shirt up, and his hardness poked and rolled against my thigh. And then he was in and I heard myself make a noise between a gasp and a sigh. He didn't have to struggle past a hymen and there was no blood — even though I considered this my first time — and when it was over, we lay beside each other like I'd always imagined I might lie with a lover some day: Happy and contented, except for the hay that poked at me through a blanket of stars.

Chapter 11

I'd been on the Pill since my first foster home, where I lived with a screaming baby and two howling toddlers.

The baby had been born addicted to crack and its high-pitched cries bored into my brain day and night. One of the toddlers had fetal alcohol syndrome. Her tiny pixie face was always hidden under masses of blond curly hair. I don't know why the third kid screamed so much. To be a pain, I guess.

Only days after I got there, they made me go to the doctor for an examination. He prodded at me with a speculum and a foot-long Q-tip while my heels hung suspended above my head. The doctor asked me questions about my sexual history, evidently forgetting I couldn't answer them. Lying across an examining table on a strip of crinkly paper, I tried to float away and think of pleasant things. When I was a really little kid and had trouble sleeping, Mama used to tuck me in at night and say, "Think of ponies and rainbows, puppies and kittens." But a more recent night, the one where my mother's boyfriend murdered Granny, still hovered fresh in my memory, and when I closed my eyes all I could see was Granny's bruised face. All I could smell was my own mother's panicked sweat. Whenever

I lay on my back, I still felt the slight weight of the silver cell phone on my chest.

After I got dressed, the doctor handed me a slip of paper without a word of comfort or instruction, perhaps assuming I was also deaf.

On the way out, the foster mother, her name was Janet, said, "We have to make sure you're safe, honey." She spoke to me slowly, her hand on my arm as we left the waiting room. I got the impression she called me "honey" because she couldn't remember my name not because she thought I was terribly sweet. I carried the car seat, where the crack baby slept. Janet secured one hand of each of the toddlers and we walked across the parking lot to her minivan. She strapped in one screaming kid and then the other. I would truly like to know where her patience came from.

She drove me to the pharmacy and I got my first wheel of birth control pills.

I had swallowed one pill every day since, round and round, wheel after wheel, needlessly. Until now. Now that I had Graydon the pills could do their magic to make sure I didn't ruin my life any more than it was already ruined.

I sat on a rock by the river holding a willow stick, poking it into the frigid muck. I watched the weight of the goo bend the stick, and then slap into the water in a glob. The late October air felt frosty all day now, not just in the mornings and evenings, and I hadn't put on enough clothes to be sitting on a rock beside a river. Great, ashen clouds covered every corner of sky, threatening cold rain.

I shivered.

Jett's steaming head sagged next to mine and I stroked it, off and on, with my other hand, when I remembered he was there.

The trees, grasses and water looked misty-pale and I imagined frogs burrowing below dark chocolate mud, preparing to enter suspended animation. The birds that stayed the winter, hardy little chickadees, nuthatches, bullying blue jays, hopped among bare branches, collecting and worrying about the coming cold.

Nacho came trotting by us and splashed straight into the river, which he loved, and got swallowed by its depth almost as soon as he stepped off the bank. He splashed around for a moment or two and then burst jauntily back onto the shore, where he shook cold droplets all over Jett. Jett jerked his head up with a look of resentment in his brown eyes. He bared his teeth and lunged at Nacho, who took an agile leap to the side. If a horse could laugh, I swear Nacho laughed at Jett as he sped back away through the field, tail tucked tight and ears pinned back.

Through my hand I giggled at Jett, who now looked as put out as a horse could look. *Poor Jett.* I tried to stroke his dove-grey nose, but he turned and walked away. *Sorry I laughed, Big Guy.*

I felt changed, stronger, and somehow less trapped. I had made a choice, and didn't regret sex with Graydon. He needed my comfort. Being needed, in turn, comforted me. In his arms, my hopes for the future had shifted enough to make me feel better about Mama.

Graydon and I now met at night in the barn at least once a week, and I had grown familiar with the hairiness of his legs, smoothness of his back, and the salty taste of his lips.

Frozen, I got off my rock, tossed the stick into the swirling river, and headed back up to the house.

"Can I hitch a ride, Lady?" called Tully. He stood on a stump in the misty field, waving at me, his red hat the only colour in the greyness of the landscape.

I smiled and backed up to the stump so Tully could crawl onto me.

"Your back's better than Char's."

I felt his cheek on my shoulder, and walked slowly, to prolong the feeling of Tully's warm weight against me.

I sat him on the paddock fence, pulled away, and turned to face him. He squinted up at me, blue eyes through wire-framed glasses.

On his face, for a moment, sat the expectant look of someone about to speak. But instead he hopped off the fence and headed for the house.

I followed.

↢⊖↢⊖↢⊖

There was a woman I'd never seen sitting on one of Mary's kitchen chairs. She wore a brown business suit that bulged plump with her flesh, like over-risen dark rye dough. Mary sat across from her wearing reading glasses and sifting through a pile of papers.

They hadn't heard me come through the back door. I was good at moving unseen and unheard, a wisp of smoke no one noticed. I crept to the staircase and sat on the bottom step, peering around the half-wall at them, but out of earshot of the conversation, no matter how hard I strained to hear. The only thing I could make out for sure was my old name on Mary's lips: Annabel.

The woman, in her suit and sensible pumps, had social services etched in every movement and gesture. She was at the farm either to talk about my mother, or Mary had called her to discuss my unfortunate run-in with the windowpanes. Either way, it couldn't be good for me.

I had seen plenty of social services types, not only the ones assigned to me, but the ones who came out to the farm for Charlene, Tully and Jerome.

Jerome's came out to the farm to pick him up. He was allowed to have visits to his parents' place one weekend every couple of months. I'd have been jealous, except it always seemed to mess him up. The visits made him sullen and quiet for a good week or so after he got back.

The stranger in the kitchen worried me. I knew I'd messed up, but I hadn't thought Mary would call social services on me. I recalled the disapproving look on her face after she had bandaged my hands and feet. I'd tried to convince myself I'd imagined it out of guilt. Since I arrived at the farm, she'd been in my corner, but I couldn't forget that look.

They couldn't make me leave. I wouldn't leave Graydon. Or Tully.

The woman gathered her papers and pushed them into a flat leather satchel. They stood in unison and shook hands, a single up-and-down pump. Mary led her to the front door and pushed the screen open for her to pass through. They smiled and nodded and the flesh under Mary's chin wobbled like a wattle.

The social services woman's ass swayed at the top of her bulbous legs, which were, in turn, perched on top of two-inch-high brown pumps. The file under her arm contained my past and my future, some of which I knew or could guess at, some of which I would probably never know.

⤞⤚⤜

I sat on my bed with my math books splayed out across it. The late afternoon sun shone through the last few autumn leaves of a backyard maple, casting my room in a warm, eerie orange light.

When I heard it, I was trying to puzzle out the answer to a geometry problem. A noise somewhere between a choke and a wheeze came through my open door from the hallway.

Alarm seized me and compelled me to the doorway for a look. I peeked down the hall but couldn't see anything. I stepped out onto the wooden floor, which creaked under my socked foot.

I could see something now. A figure lay on the floor by the top of the stairs. I got closer and saw Jerome. Ah, Jerome, kidding around. But no, he wasn't kidding around this time. I had never seen anything like it; his face was a dusky shade of blue and his eyes were rolled up into his skull.

An emergency. But what did I need to do? Mary had made us all take one of those first-aid courses. I needed to calm down and figure out what was happening? If he was choking, I was sure I couldn't lift up his bulky body to do the Heimlich manoeuvre on him. And then I remembered the allergy. I had to find the little pen thing that would stop his reaction. I put my hand on Jerome's chest while I leapt around him and down the stairs, but I'm not sure he noticed my reassurance.

I hauled open the kitchen cupboard where Mary kept the bandages, antiseptic spray, Tylenol and stuff like that. In my panic, I pulled everything out onto the counter and there, in the middle of all the junk, was the little plastic cylinder with Jerome's medicine in it. I grabbed it and ran, but wasn't even at the foot of the stairs when I heard Char scream.

On the way up toward her, I gestured for her to call an ambulance, but she stood there with her hands over her mouth and jogged her knees up and down. Before I touched Jerome, I took her shoulders and shook her hard. She gasped and ran off to her room. She had an extension in there and I hoped to God she was calling 911.

I popped open the medicine cap and pulled out the device. While I turned it in my hands I refused to look at Jerome's face, terrified that what I might see there would make me mess up.

When I figured out which end had the needle, I went for it and pushed it into the fabric of his track pants. Afterward, I lay across him crying for what seemed like an age, unsure whether he would live or die, when Tully came running up the stairs.

"Oh my God. What's going on?"

I looked up at him.

"Holy cow. Is Jerome…okay?"

I was sure he almost asked if he was dead. I sat back and we both looked at him. He seemed to be breathing, but his swollen face was still an odd colour.

"Did you push in the Epipen?"

I nodded.

"I think he's okay. I think you did it."

We sat together on the stairs listening to Jerome's rasping breath.

And then events rushed together and got blurred in commotion. Ambulance attendants barreled through the door, Mary came hobbling in from outside shrieking and scared, Tully and I got pushed back and away.

When it was all done, Jerome and Mary were gone, a mess of medical junk littered the stairs, Char refused to come out of her room, Bobby sat distraught at the kitchen table waiting for the phone to ring, and no one knew where Graydon was.

⌖⌖⌖

The most Mary said in the next week was that Jerome was going to be fine.

"This sucks. It's Jerome's night to clear the table." Tully whispered to me while he rattled the dishes together into a small pile. No one else spoke about it; but Tully and I, at least, missed Jerome and wondered when he would come back.

Bobby got up from the table and took a forlorn stretch. "I'm going out to the shop." He seemed lost without his shadow.

Char and Graydon seemed unaffected. Char recovered from the scare quickly, even beginning to brag about her role in saving his life.

Mary had always been so careful. Aside from when Jerome might be coming back, the only other thing I continued to wonder was where the hell did the peanut butter come from? For sure Jerome would never touch peanuts on purpose.

Every time I left my room to make out with Graydon, I got as nervous as if I were about to go onstage. Not that I'd ever been onstage, but I imagined that kind of nervousness was what it would feel like.

Getting ready was a ritual: fussing with my hopeless hair, selecting the right clothes, picking out either light blue jeans or dark blue, the red plaid work shirt or the green. And I liked to wear Char's strawberry lip gloss. I vowed to buy my own the next time we went to town, but until then I was stuck stealing hers.

It was tricky, taking the gloss from her room and putting it back without her knowing. If she ever found it missing, she'd go ballistic and I'd be dead meat. Who else would she blame but me?

Listening hard was the key. Char tended toward laziness and sloppiness, and that made her noisy. So I could tell when she was in her room by standing outside the door for a few minutes, listening.

It was ten-thirty at night, not too early for a clandestine lip gloss raid and not too late. Get in, get out. Most likely, Char was downstairs watching television with the others. I leaned against the wall beside her door, pretending to examine my fingernails, in case anyone happened by. I didn't hear anything for a full two minutes. I timed it.

I whipped into her room as quickly as I could. Almost at her dresser, my hand outstretched, I heard a noise. In an instant I had the gloss and was on my hands and knees, letting myself feel briefly impressed at my quick reflexes.

I had just about decided that the noise was my imagination when I glanced into the closet and saw Char on her knees, rocking back and forth and making faint retching noises into what looked like a re-sealable plastic baggie. She had done her hair up in a clasp to keep it out of her face.

Good God, Jerome had been right all along. Char was anorexic, or bulimic, or some kind of "ick" that they warned us against becoming in health class. I was in awe that anyone could throw up so quietly. The time I had caught stomach flu, I had retched, spluttered and gasped so loudly, Granny had to apologize to the neighbours for me making them feel sick.

I was crawling my silent way to freedom when Char looked right at me. I stopped. We stared at each other. I couldn't look away or move. She didn't seem surprised or embarrassed, as I had expected she would. She looked frank, like she dared me to tell.

We stared so long that my eyes started to water, so I looked away and left her room.

I took the lip gloss with me, but I didn't go back and return it. Char never said anything about the gloss, but I never gave it back and never wore it again either.

⇜⇝⇜

It was in the last stall in the stable, after midnight, that I felt alive and truly safe. This time Graydon had a large plastic bottle of cola instead of liquor and he was pouring it out into cups for us to share. Cola was another thing Mary disapproved of and wouldn't keep in the house. So this felt like a royal treat.

When I took a sip, the bubbles fizzed through my nostrils and clung to the fine hairs that lined my upper lip.

"You know what went on tonight?" he asked.

I shook my head.

"Tonight everyone went to the school dance."

I recalled the posters that lined the hallways near my locker. I shrugged. So what? The last thing I wanted to do was go to a dance full of people who'd spit on me as soon as look at me.

"We should've been there. We have a right to go to a dance like everybody else."

He had a point. Strictly speaking, we *were* allowed to go. Mary and Bobby would let us, as long as we got home by curfew and agreed not to do anything stupid like get drunk or high. But going to a dance felt like suicide to me. The other kids would kill us. Maybe not literally but definitely socially. I couldn't even picture me or Tully or Char standing in the darkened gym, music playing, a glitter ball casting star-dot reflections against the walls and ceiling, like I'd seen in movies. I could imagine Graydon there. People didn't mess with him the way they messed with the rest of us. I wondered if he felt like we held him back, stigmatized him with how clearly different we were. Fitting in at high school was about being the same, not about being different.

Out of nowhere, he clapped his hands together loudly and I nearly jumped out of my skin.

"I got an idea." He leaned back on his bale of hay and fished around in the front pocket of his ski jacket until he pulled out a cell phone. "We'll call for pizza. I got some money in my wallet and I know an all-night pizza place."

I bet that was how he got hold of the rum. Maybe the person who'd got him the phone also supplied him with liquor. But if a pizza guy rang the doorbell at the house at one in the morning, we'd be busted for sure.

I grabbed for the phone. Graydon stepped up onto the hay bale and held it high above his head.

"Come on. I'll tell the driver to make sure he delivers it to the barn, not the house."

There were no guarantees. I jumped up and almost got it. He laughed and leapt to another bale farther away. I pursued him and he ran in a circle until I was running around after him.

"All right, you win." He kissed me and then slipped the phone back into his pocket. "I won't call."

I made a "phew" gesture by wiping my brow with my hand. We collapsed, giggling, in a pile on the floor. He kissed me again, longer now that we'd got our breath back. I tangled my fingers in his hair. He swept his palms around my waist to my shoulder blades, my shirt riding up above my ribs.

We were off.

Chapter 12

On Sunday Tully and I were on after-dinner dish duty. Steam rose from the bubbles, a witch's brew of lemon-scented soap. I thrust my bare hands into the water and fished out a long serrated knife; I hated wearing rubber gloves because of the chemical stink they left on my skin even after I tried to wash it off.

We were alone in the kitchen and Tully had that expectant look on his face, the same one he'd had when he sat on the fence rail, like he was about to say something significant. Finally, he did say something.

"So, you and Graydon, huh?" His voice wavered slightly.

I let the knife slip back into the water and turned fast to face him. My wet hands went to my hips, soaking through my sweater onto the skin at my waist. I put a so-what's-it-to-you look on my face.

Tully swallowed. "Remember when Char said he was trouble? Well, I agree. I think he's dangerous and you should be careful."

My insides became a seething cauldron of anger. I suddenly couldn't bear the pleading, reasonable look on Tully's face. I turned my back on him and stomped out of the kitchen to my room.

Who was he to lecture me? Tully was afraid of his own shadow and wouldn't take a chance if his life depended on it. I had decided to take a chance and he was jealous. Jealous of our relationship because he wanted one of his own, and jealous because I had dared to do something that didn't involve him.

⬦⬦⬦

School sucked, as always. Not the classes or the work, or even most of the teachers. All the crap came from the atmosphere and the other students' expectations. It felt like people wanted something from me all the time. I needed to be cool and popular, wear the right clothes and use the right expressions; but I was hopeless.

Because I couldn't speak they didn't know what I had in my head. I couldn't feel comfortable in anything other than jeans, sneakers and big flannel shirts. I didn't want to grow my hair or dye it, wear nail polish or heels. Femininity held no interest for me; in fact, I hated the whole concept of it. I didn't know specifically what I was afraid of, but exposing my new curves by wearing something tight-fitting gave me a bad case of stomach butterflies.

Each of us from Noble Spirit suffered. Everyone knew we were foster kids, and it didn't matter how cool we tried to be, we were molded by the foster kids cookie cutter and couldn't change shape.

None of us shared classes. Char, Graydon and Tully were older than me and in the next grade. Jerome took remedial classes, I took advanced, and now he was gone anyway. I had a special exemption — recommended by the psychiatrist who interviewed me when my mother was in jail — that got me out of oral presentations. Thank God. Otherwise we would all have been treated to me standing silent in front of a class of mocking faces for twenty minutes.

If Noble Spirit kids found one another at lunch, we ate together. If not, we didn't. After lunch and during free periods, I hid in a corner of the library.

One Friday in November, I was making notes for a history essay about Jacques Cartier when Graydon slipped into the chair beside me.

"Want to meet me tonight?" He might as well have said, 'Want a million dollars and a house in the south of France'?

I nodded. I was OTR. That meant On The Rag, an expression I picked up from listening in on conversations in the school ladies' room. If I ever got my voice back, I'd be ready to be cool.

I planned to deal with the OTR problem later that night. He squeezed my hand under the table and I squeezed his hand back. I felt like I was getting less awkward with physical touch. I was trying, anyway.

Graydon winked and left the table. I looked back to my pages of careful Cartier notes and began doodling in the margins.

Like always, I left the house a few minutes before midnight, dressed super warmly in my winter coat, my gloves, hat and boots to get across to the stable. Granny used to say we Canadians turned into onions in the winter, with our layers upon layers of clothing.

November had sprung up colder than usual and the sky had decided to decorate by spreading a thin layer of snow across the rutted earth, vanilla frosting on a chocolate cake.

Instead of waiting in the last stall, Graydon met me at the stable door.

"Let's change it up."

He took my hand and led me into the hay barn. I climbed to the loft using the wooden ladder that Bobby had built, and Graydon clattered up behind me. He had one of the battery-powered space heaters whirring away, and a camp lantern for light. I shed my gloves into the pockets of my winter jacket and then took that off too. He laid me across a bed that was spread with harvest gold, and when I closed my eyes I smelled a field and saw hay waving hello on summer wind.

The sensation of the prickly hay against my back, coupled with his soft hand under my turtleneck gave me an abrupt jolt of ticklishness and I laughed. He stifled me with a hot kiss. I giggled around his lips and he laughed too.

Graydon's hands had almost got as far as my jeans' fly, which was when I planned to stop him because of OTR, and make him a replacement offer he wouldn't refuse, when I heard a sudden whoosh through the barn board walls that sounded too real to be the passion that pounded in my ears. The noise had panic in it.

I struggled away from Graydon and crawled on my knees to the tiny loft window.

"Hey! What're you doing?"

Beyond webs of frost on the pane, I caught sight of a faint orange glow. Frozen by sudden indecision, I stared and gaped through the glass, my hot palm cooling against it.

"Oh shit." Graydon's voice was like a hypnotist's finger snap in my ear.

I fumbled for my jacket, pushed my arms into the sleeves, and yanked at Graydon to follow. I charged frontward down the ladder as if it were a flight of stairs, and out the door. In the open, the scent of smoke rode the cold air. I ran around the building until I got a good view of the stable. Smoke danced like a celebration around the roof, an errant flame licking high every now and then.

My eyes watered with cold and alarm.

The horses. I hoped to God they were all outside. But what if one of them got forgotten? Who checked the barn? It hadn't been me.

I ran to the stable door and straight through, panic making me terrified and fearless at the same time. What if Jett were inside? What would I do without him?

It was hot inside but there were no flames. Only light smoke, swaying and dancing like it forgot it belonged to the inferno on the roof. Barely aware of Graydon grabbing at my jacket, trying to pull me out, I checked every stall. When I knew for sure they were all empty, I stumbled back out into the cold night, and Graydon's warm arms.

I moved away from him, turned toward the house, aiming to run in and wake Mary to call 911. I felt Graydon's hands grip my upper arms and his face swam toward mine.

"Run with me. Now."

I screwed my face into a question and tried to pull away from him.

"Mary'll be pretty angry. Here we are, out in the middle of the night, in violation of the rules. But that's not the worst of it. What if she blames you?"

I stopped struggling to get his hands off me, and stared into his smoky eyes.

"She knows you have that lighter, Ghost. And you've done some crazy shit. Remember the windows? She'll send you away if she thinks you set that building on fire, and we might never see each other again."

I shook my head while my heart disassembled and reassembled his words. What if he was right? I might lose everyone I cared about in one swoop. They had already taken Jerome. What about Mary, Bobby, Tully, Graydon? I thought of the social services woman at Mary's kitchen table with her papers and the pieces of my future they might have contained. I'd lost so much; I had to hang onto something. Someone.

"I'll run with you," he said. "We can be together."

I glanced back at the house. A light winked on in Mary and Bobby's window.

"Look, they're up. They'll be calling the fire department right now. Everyone'll be safe. But after it all settles, there'll be blame. There always is."

I hadn't done anything worse than have sex with my boyfriend after curfew. But how would I prove that? I couldn't even tell my side of the story. Graydon was right. I had the lighter, and I'd been stupid and impulsive when I'd broken the glass. I'd disappointed Mary and turned my back on Tully. If they cast me out I'd be without even Graydon. I would finally shatter, for real.

He let go of me and I stood swaying. Nothing was stopping me from taking whichever course I chose.

He put out his hand and I took it.

We ran.

Chapter 13

A t the side of the deserted road in the dark, I felt a bitter chill that came from more than the frigid air.

After we had stumbled along pathways through woods and fields, we reached the Second Line Road. Second Line split farmland north to south from Old Carp Road all the way to Dunrobin. It felt like we were heading south, toward town, but in the bleak rural darkness and my pulsing panic, I couldn't be sure.

Graydon put his hand on my arm and stopped me by the side of the road.

"We need help," he said.

I shivered and sobbed, my breath steaming out and disappearing into the country night.

He pulled the cell phone out of his jacket pocket and dialed. "Hey. Yeah, man. Second Line Road. Like, south of Old Carp Road. I don't know. Drive the whole way along. We're here. We'll keep walking. And hurry up. It's freezing."

He slid the phone back into his jacket and nudged me forward. He tried to keep his arm around me while we walked, but we tripped over each other's feet. Instead we trudged along side by side. I had my arms wrapped around me so hard they ached, and an ice-mask of frozen tears numbed my face.

In the headlights of a passing truck, a shadow of myself appeared in front of me, stretching out on the dirty snow like a demonic third person. The red lights crested a ridge and disappeared down the other side. I pushed my numb legs forward, trying to think about nothing. Trying to make my mind as blank as a piece of white paper. *Don't think.*

Another vehicle rumbled up from behind, casting a new version of my shadow self, but this time, after the car passed, it pulled to the side of the road. The taillights cast a pale dirty glow across the ground. We hustled up alongside the car.

A man in the driver's seat spoke through the automatic passenger window, which squeaked on its way down. "So, you kids need a ride somewhere, eh?"

"Do we ever," said Graydon, pushing me in front of him, toward the car.

"Get on in."

Graydon reached around me and pulled the door open with a pop. The air inside oozed over me, a warm maple syrup feeling. I'd never paid much attention to cars, but this was some kind of old boat of a sedan. Probably screwed together exactly a day after power windows first got invented.

I took a picture in my head in the brief moment of light before Graydon slammed the door behind us. The wide bench seats, covered in burgundy fabric, looked scarred and worn. The plastic that lined the inside of the backseat doors had cracks and jagged holes.

"You came quick. Thanks, man," said Graydon when the car had moved back onto the road. "It's fucking cold outside."

I winced at the curse. What if this guy took offense and chucked us back into the snow?

"No problem. You gonna introduce me?"

"Yeah, man," Graydon said. "Sure thing. Ghost, this is Cooper. He's a friend of mine."

Cooper put the car in gear and we rolled off onto the road. I looked at the back of his basketball head. It swayed to one side and then the other as the car followed the curves of the yellow line. He looked older than Graydon. Definitely not a high school kid. Who was this guy and how did Graydon know him?

"Where are we headed, Cooper?"

"Downtown Ottawa."

"Sounds good." Graydon relaxed and settled back into the seat beside me.

Now that my body was no longer in motion, my hands fell to trembling and I could barely suck in breath around my sobs. We had already travelled from the narrow country lane to the better-lit, wider road that led to the highway.

"You guys okay?" asked Cooper, while glimpses of his concerned brow in the rearview mirror flashed off and on with the passing streetlamps.

"Don't worry. We're good." Graydon put an arm around my shoulder and pulled me into him. I breathed, listened to my heartbeat, and watched the lights from oncoming cars and trucks flood the interior of the car and then pass away.

The warmth that had at first seemed so inviting, now felt sickly hot and itchy. I rubbed my forehead with my palms and the moisture drained away from my swollen tongue. I gripped Graydon's knee and shook it urgently.

"Uh, you better pull over, there, Cooper."

"Huh?"

"Pull over. Quick. I think she's gonna be sick."

The car hadn't quite come to a stop when I scrambled over Graydon's thighs and my hands and knees slammed onto the frozen dirt. My stomach retched steaming bile on the cold gravel shoulder of the road. The ground underneath me was frozen hard but bare of snow.

Graydon stood beside me and waited until I was done.

I crawled back into the car and lay my head in Graydon's lap. The one advantage of short hair was that vomit tended not to get stuck in it.

"Hey, you guys have someplace to stay?" asked Cooper.

"No, man."

"I got a place with an extra bedroom no one's using," Cooper said.

"That's awful generous," Graydon said. "I think we'll do that."

I worried. I didn't know anything about this guy or his place. Graydon stroked my hair and I think I slept.

The brakes squealed and I sat up, dazed with leftover shock, my mouth pasty.

Somehow, I had expected downtown at night to be like daylight, but instead this street looked grainy with dimness. I slid across the seat and out of the car after Graydon, and we followed Cooper to a pale blue door that seemed to grow right up out of the sidewalk. There was no step in front of it, and the door leaned to one side at a weird angle.

Cooper fumbled with keys that jangled out into a night too dark to see by, but too bright to view the stars. Graydon held me in what felt like a headlock, as if he wanted to make sure I would neither run off nor fall to the ground in a heap.

The rubber seal around the door made a whoosh as Cooper pushed it open. He had to duck to go through the doorframe because he must have been way over six feet tall, at least halfway to seven feet. Graydon and I followed.

Cooper led us down a short set of concrete steps into a tiny vestibule with two more doors. The space smelled vaguely of shoe polish and boiled cabbage. Each door had a bell on the wall next to the knob, with a number stuck above it. After another jolly tinkle from Cooper's set of keys, we shuffled into number 2.

The apartment stank of old take-out food — Chinese chicken balls and pizza — and my stomach lurched. My legs were rubbery with weariness and I fell onto a long couch lavishly patterned in unidentifiable stains.

"Come on, let's get you into bed," said Graydon. "Thanks for letting us crash here, Cooper."

He picked me up and carried me through one of the doors along the right wall, pulled off my boots and coat, and tucked me into the bed.

"You okay?" he asked.

I nodded but I wasn't okay.

"I'm not tired yet, so I'm gonna stay up a bit longer and talk to Cooper for a while. Get some sleep and you'll feel better about things tomorrow."

He kissed my forehead, flipped off the light and backed out the door, leaving me to the foreign darkness.

The smell of the mouldy sheets and pillow already clung to my head and the hairs inside my nose. My eyes adjusted to the dark and I could see the four bare walls around me. A closet along the right-hand wall had wooden bi-fold doors with horizontal slats. Some of the slats had broken off, making the doors look like the evil grin of a jack o' lantern in the dark.

Positive I'd never be able to sleep, I stared at a long crack in the ceiling that was so deep it looked bottomless, like a chasm.

◦◦◦◦◦◦

I woke to the sound of low chatter, clinking glass, and a murmur of laughter. My bladder felt like it had swollen to the size of a cantaloupe, aching and threatening to burst when I moved.

Lemon-curd fingers of light reached through the window of the room I had slept in. The air outside the sheets and blankets made my nose raw with cold.

Unwilling to leave the mildewed sheets now that they shared my body's warmth, I wrapped them around me and shuffled out the bedroom door.

"She's alive!" Graydon said theatrically when he saw me.

I bounced my knees up and down and crossed my legs in an awkward but unmistakable need-a-pee dance. With obvious amusement he pointed at the door to my left. The bathroom was small but when I sat on the toilet I noticed it had a full-sized tub and a sink with a counter. The mirror above the sink housed a medicine cabinet. Before I washed my hands I opened it, more so I wouldn't have to look at my reflection than to see what it had inside. The rusty shelf held only a razor and can of shaving cream.

When I came back out, I joined Graydon on the couch, wrapping the sheet close around me and pushing my feet under his thigh.

The place had an underground, abandoned feeling. The room seemed temporary, as if it waited for the current occupant to either make it a home or leave. The top edge of the bare windows — narrow and oblong — touched the ceiling, which made the empty, smudged walls seem to go on forever. Each rectangle of glass revealed only the cinderblock of the building alongside.

The apartment's corners held grey shadows and greasy smells.

"You want a beer?" asked Cooper. Graydon waggled his half-finished bottle in front of me by way of encouragement. I noticed that Labatt's Blue bottles, empty and cinnamon-tinted, littered the linoleum floor.

I looked around for a clock but didn't see one. My internal chronometer whispered early morning. Hardly beer time, but I nodded anyway.

"Excellent." Cooper went off and clattered around in the fridge. I heard a spurt as he twisted off the cap. He returned and handed me the steaming beer.

They had both drunk enough not to realize the time. I didn't want to know, or care, about time either. I took a big gulp and it fizzed up my nose. I coughed and spluttered. They laughed. Jerks.

I wiped foam and spittle off my face and watched while Cooper and Graydon ignored me, and settled into easy conversation, a skill that had always eluded me — even when I'd had a voice. I set my beer bottle on the floor, unfinished.

I shifted on the couch and got poked in the hip by something hard. When I pulled Graydon's plastic lighter out of my pocket I felt immediately pale and sick.

All threads of reason dropped from my mind in an instant and I thought, *what if I did set that fire and didn't remember doing it?* The memory of breaking the panes of glass had become dream-like and hazy, as if I only watched while someone else threw those rocks. Maybe my mind had gone a step further and completely blocked out the memory of setting that fire.

But that was crazy; I wouldn't do that. I wouldn't risk a horse's life. I knew that much about myself. But did Mary know that about me? I never said a word to her in all our time together. Going back might mean facing Mary's accusing eyes. I was too scared of her disappointment to think about going back.

The fire could have been an accident, what with all that hay and straw. I'd read about spontaneous combustion. It might have been a combination of horse manure gas, tinder of dry hay, and ancient grey barn boards. A coincidence.

Graydon wanted to be with me. That was real. I didn't have Mary anymore, but at least I had Graydon. He would look after me.

A hunger pang clenched my stomach and a rumble interrupted the air.

"Holy hell!" Graydon said, his voice pink and round with beer. "You hungry or what? I'm hungry too. Cooper? What do you say we get a pizza or something?"

"I'm up for that, but I think it's about nine or ten in the morning. There's a cheap breakfast place we can walk to from here. Eggs, bacon, coffee and shit like that."

Graydon clapped his hands and rubbed them together. "Let's do it."

The greasy spoon breakfast place was cheap, but mostly good. In my hunger, I ate three scrambled eggs, sausages, bacon and hash browns, which were raw in the middle, but I ate them anyway.

"She's a machine," said Cooper. "I never seen a girl eat so much."

Graydon put an arm around me, proud, as if he were responsible for my extraordinary ability to eat an enormous amount of food. Cooper left the table to go to the washroom and Graydon grabbed my hand and leaned in to kiss it.

"You better now?"

I nodded.

"You know there's no going back, right? It's you and me now, but don't worry. I'll look after you. I promise." His grey eyes had a hint of green while they searched for my loyalty. I nodded again and he smiled.

I rested my head on his shoulder and he squeezed my hand tight, his face in my hair, warm breath on my scalp.

"You're my girl," he whispered.

When Cooper loped back to the table and slid onto the bench seat, Graydon let me go.

"I'll get this one, Coop," said Graydon when the bill came. He pulled a wad of money out of his back pocket and counted out a couple of fives. I wondered where he'd got all the money. Had Cooper given it to him? He might have always had it. There wasn't much need for money on the farm. I realized how little I knew about Graydon.

"Thanks, man." Cooper pulled a knitted toque over his shaved head. He smiled with a row of perfect white teeth, the kind of dazzling set you could catch on a toothpaste ad.

We went back out onto the street and got blasted with cold air. Downtown Ottawa looked dingy under a sun blocked by a sheet of haze, like a flashlight struggling to shine through waxed paper.

Back in the apartment, which didn't feel much warmer than outside, the guys hit a wall made of all-night beers and greasy food, and collapsed onto the furniture.

"Shit man, I'm bagged," said Graydon.

"Me too. Listen Gray, I got a little contract job tomorrow painting the main floor rooms of a fancy house out in the 'burbs. You want in, and I'll split the money with ya?"

"Sure. I hate painting, but if I can make a buck, I'll do it."

"We'll be done quick if we do it together. One coat tomorrow, next coat the day after. Bingo, we're done."

I smiled at Graydon. Only one day out on our own, and he already had a job. We were going to be okay. I didn't know how

Cooper fit in, but I knew Graydon would tell me sometime. I was sure.

"I'll tell you one other thing we can do to earn our keep around here." Graydon winked at me before he continued. "Ghost cooks. She can buy some decent food and make us nice dinners."

"No shit," said Cooper. "Sounds good."

I felt a surge of panic.

Graydon said he and Cooper were going to have a nap, handed me forty dollars, and sent me out to buy groceries. Graydon asked him where the store was and Cooper mumbled something on his way to bed, his hand spiralling meaninglessly in the air.

I stood on the sidewalk in front of the blue apartment door and looked up and down the street, unsure of which way I ought to go.

An expanse of sidewalk, like a wide concrete field, stretched out in front of the National Gallery, an awesome glass and steel structure that overlooked the river. The gallery behind me, I stood looking across the street at the most impressive church I'd ever seen. Two spires spiked into the clouds on either side of a huge window the shape of the pope's hat. On the peak of the roof, between those majestic spires, stood a golden statue that might have been the Virgin Mary. The church looked ancient and loved.

Granny would have adored it. She hadn't been religious, but she was a traditionalist, and felt affection for most of the trappings of Western culture — with the exception of birthdays. She believed wedding and funeral services should be held in a church like that one.

Granny had her final service in the funeral home chapel, a stuffy room with a red carpet, uncomfortable chairs, and the smell of dusty plastic flowers and candle wax. She would have been disappointed.

Mama hadn't come to Granny's funeral because she was in jail. I wondered if Mama would have come if she could. I wasn't sure she would have.

A social worker named Mona, who I'd met only the day before, held my hand while a man who'd never set eyes on Granny's living face said a word or two about her. He was short and had shiny black hair that looked like a helmet, hard like black plastic. I imagined him taking it off his head when he arrived home and hanging it on a peg by the door. White spittle formed in the corners of his mouth while he spoke.

I wished Mona would let go of my hand.

The plain wooden casket remained closed, and for the life of me I couldn't imagine Granny inside it. Instead, I imagined her floating over my head, telling me off for wearing pants to her funeral, instead of a dress or even a nice skirt. Those blasted expectations could reach beyond the grave. When Mona finally let my hand go, I wiped my wet palms down the thighs of my pants.

Granny's old friend Olga sat in the row of seats in front of us. She looked small and grey, kind of curled up at the edges. Because Olga was there, Granny's life seemed somehow more real.

After the service, Olga came up to me.

"Oh, Annabel. What will I do?"

I looked down at her, not sure what she wanted from me. I was too busy wondering what *I* would do.

"Margaret was a wonderful friend," she said. "And she was so proud of you. Always going on about how clever you were in school. 'She will go far, that one. Mark my words.' That was what she said. I had to ask her if we could talk about something other than you."

I hadn't known. Granny had been proud of me. Why had she never told me?

The funeral wasn't like in the books I had read. After the church service, no one took me to any gravesite for a burial. I didn't get to stand around a hole in the ground in the mournful rain and scream at the merciless heavens. Mona walked me out the funeral home door, my feet swimming in sweat inside my patent leather shoes. I got in a car with her and we drove away. That was it. No one told me I was supposed to have said my goodbyes to Granny right then and there, or I would have. I didn't care where Granny's body had gone; I wanted the ritual of the ceremony, like she would've wanted.

I did wonder, though, where my grandfather's money had got to. To hear Mama tell it, there had been a lot. Whenever Mama came to the apartment, she begged Granny for some of that money, but Granny never budged toward giving her any. I could see Granny's point. But maybe there wasn't money, for whatever reason, because I never saw it. Our frugal lives had moved onward in that small apartment without anything new, with Granny melting the nubs of my crayons together rather than buying a fresh pack.

Graydon's forty dollars still sat in my back pocket. I hadn't come across a grocery store yet. The day had warmed and I began to like exploring these new streets. The smells here were not the subtle green scents of the farm, but were more like military assaults, grey plumes of exhaust smoke and garbage from down the alleyways. I decided that was okay. But if I had smelled horse manure or a field, I probably would have cried.

To my surprise, everywhere I walked reminded me of Tully: the big-box bookstore on a corner, a trendy children's clothing shop with stuff in the window that looked his size, an optician's with a display of beautiful frames. Tully needed new glasses; I could tell when he looked into the distance. I pictured him standing on the bottom fence rail squinting toward the horizon, looking for the last horse to come in for breakfast. I almost heard his whistle. Tully could put a pinky finger of each hand to his lips and whistle so loud it'd make your ears ring. Tully showed me how he curled his tongue up and put the V of his fingers under it, closed his lips, and blew. I tried and tried but all I could make was air and spit.

I walked down streets, turned a few corners, got lost and panicky for a moment or two, and finally found a grocery store.

How was I supposed to know what to get? I had no plan. I'd gone with Mary to the grocery store, and I used to go with Granny too, but hadn't paid attention like I'd be doing it myself one day. I threw stuff in the cart that I had seen on the shelves at the farm — loaf of bread, jar of grape jelly, cans of tomato sauce. I had to be careful that the total wouldn't be more than the money I had with me.

Being voiceless in the city turned out to be okay. The checkout girl didn't look at me twice when I acknowledged her "Hey, how ya doin'?" with only a nod. She didn't ask me any real questions, just bagged my food and handed me my change.

I left the store with plastic bags full of meat and produce that I hoped I could turn into a few meals. I also bought a box of condoms for Graydon to use, having gone on the lam without my birth control. My life was screwed up enough without making that kind of mistake.

Standing on the sidewalk, bags in hand, I discovered that Cooper's apartment was only two streets away. I should have turned left instead of right from the start.

Chapter 14

It ended up taking the rest of the week for Graydon and Cooper to finish their painting job. While they were out, I stayed home alone.

Cooper had a magnetic sign that read, *The Cooper Painting Company*, with his phone number underneath. He stuck it on the door of his decrepit car whenever he went to a job, I supposed in the hope that a passerby might hire him on for more work. One night I was looking at the sign, curled against the wall by the door, when I noticed the phone number was one digit short. I didn't point it out to him because, well, so what? I wondered if he'd messed it up on purpose or if he was just careless. Maybe this painting business was a sham.

On the morning of my first day, I left the apartment and walked down a few blocks where I discovered a used bookstore. I peered through the glass at some sun-faded hard covers. I walked into the musty shop and felt a calm that came with being surrounded by books and paper. A rack at the front of the store had some paperbacks on display and I plucked out a bunch that looked interesting.

I paid my five bucks and the mousy man behind the counter began shoving them, one by one, into a plastic grocery bag.

"This one's good." He held up *Heart of Darkness* and peered at me with a look in his pouchy eyes that might have been curiosity or a head cold. "Interesting choice. You must be studying it in school."

I shook my head. He slipped in the last book and handed me the bag.

"What's your name?"

Don't mind me, I'm only a Ghost. I smiled, bit my thumb and walked out. He probably thought I was being coy. Let him.

Graydon gave me some money for clothes. I had run from Noble Spirit with nothing, not even a change of underwear, so that's what I bought next: a package of six pairs from the thrift store. I also found two pairs of army pants, one olive and the other beige, and two shirts, one faded blue denim, one dark blue denim, and a package of thick socks. With the clothes I already had, that made three outfits, plus underwear and socks for a week. What more could a girl ask for?

I carried my bags back to Cooper's apartment and let myself in with the spare key he'd let me have. I stood in the loneliness of silent walls, feeling dazed, as if I were hovering between the faded linoleum and stained ceiling. My body twirled in midair, my gaze taking in the nasty corner kitchen, front door, bathroom, first bedroom, second bedroom.

In only a moment, things felt more solid. I walked to the kitchen and searched the fridge and cupboards for what I might make for dinner.

I had never been responsible for making a whole meal myself, so the prospect felt adventurous, even pioneering. I was a pioneer woman, waiting for the men to return from a hard day at the sawmill, or the wheat fields, or wherever pioneers used to go out and work.

I had a package of noodles, a jar of tomato sauce and some hamburger meat. That definitely sounded like the makings of something. Pioneer spaghetti and meatballs.

Mary had always broken an egg into the meat and added breadcrumbs. I didn't have breadcrumbs, but I had a loaf of bread. I broke the bread into bits with my fingers and put it in a dented metal bowl with the egg and ground meat. Gagging, I mashed it together with my hands. The stuff in the bowl looked, and felt, like I imagined cold guts might look and feel. I transformed it into small pinkish balls that sat on the counter like they were waiting for me to get a cue and play pool.

I turned on the television to check the time on the weather channel: four o'clock.

Graydon had told me they'd be home by six, so at five-thirty I filled the biggest pot I could find (which wasn't very big) with water and set it on to boil. I dumped the jar of sauce into a saucepan and plopped in the meatballs.

With the noodles in the pot, and everything simmering on the stove, homey and warm, I felt pretty domestic.

While I waited, I discovered my spirit wanted someone else to come through the door, not Graydon and Cooper, not even my distant mother, who had finally stopped invading my dreams. I wanted Tully to come, be proud of my accomplishment and eat what I had cooked. His praise would have turned me inside out with pleasure.

I was well into reading one of my new paperbacks when Graydon and Cooper traipsed in, covered in daubs of sage green paint, looking sweaty and exhausted.

"Smells great, Ghost!" said Graydon. "I told you she'd cook us up a fine meal."

"Gotta admit, it smells pretty good in here."

Graydon kissed me with damp lips and stripped off his outer layer of clothing. While Cooper had a shower we made out on the couch. Then Graydon showered and Cooper nosed around in the kitchen, peering under pot lids and sniffing.

"Hey, did you stir any of this stuff?"

I went to kitchen and plucked a cracked wooden spoon out of one of the drawers. When I stuck it into the rumbling pasta pot, I discovered half the water had boiled away and the noodles were congealed into a solid mass in the centre of the pot. The sauce had an inch-thick layer of grease on top and stuck to the bottom of the pan when I tried to scrape the spoon through it. I had not created a culinary masterpiece. I'd created a disaster.

"You cooked those meatballs and drained the fat before you put them in the sauce, right?" asked Cooper.

I blinked at him.

"Are you retarded as well as dumb, Freakazoid?"

His words shocked me. If he was so smart, he should have cooked the meal. I felt wretched and useless. I could probably kill us all with food poisoning. Right then, death sounded pretty good.

Graydon came out of the bathroom with a small white towel across his loins, looking confident and beautiful through my angry tears.

"Jesus, Ghost, what's wrong?"

"She fucked up the dinner," said Cooper.

"It's okay." Graydon took me in his arms. "We'll eat it no matter what."

"Eat it? It's all fucked up."

"Cooper, you're gonna eat it."

"Oh sure. I'll dump the noodles out on the counter. We can slice them like a loaf of bread."

Graydon looked in the pots. "It's fine. Don't worry. I'll fix it. We can boil another batch of pasta and that'll give the meatballs some time to cook right through. I'll skim the grease off the sauce."

"But I'm starving, man."

"Go chew on a beer and shut up."

I didn't want Graydon to have to fix it. I wanted it to have been perfect the first time. I wanted Cooper to go away and for this place to be ours alone.

I shut myself in the second bedroom until I heard Graydon's soft tapping.

"Can I come in?"

I opened the door.

"Dinner's ready and it's fine. Thank you for making it."

I lay back on the bed and covered my face with my hands. He took one hand and pulled me up with it.

Graydon was different Out Here than he had been at Noble Spirit. At the farm he was distant and aloof, even when we were alone together. Here he acted more attentive, seemed to care about me more. I got the idea he was afraid of being Out Here as much as I was.

"Come and eat with us." He took me to the living room and sat me on the couch. The bowl of spaghetti he placed in my lap looked okay.

"Eat up."

We ate in silence. The sauce needed salt, but was otherwise choke-down-able. During the meal, I caught resentful looks from Cooper while he swigged from his beer bottle.

I didn't care about him, with his perfect teeth and cue-ball head. But I vowed to do better next time, for Graydon.

The bathroom smelled of the sulphur of a match, lit and extinguished. When I shook out the contents of the dented metal wastebasket — empty toilet rolls and snot rags — I noticed the can had scorch marks up the insides. I took a scrub brush to it in the kitchen sink but the black marks stubbornly hung on.

The marks were a mystery that I didn't have the headspace to worry about. My brain was filled to brimming with worry about Tully, Jerome, Mary and the horses. And me. I worried about me and felt sorry for myself.

Reading was my only real distraction. Lyle at the bookstore would trade different used paperbacks for ones I'd already finished, if I took them back. His store was my lending library without me needing a card. I didn't know why he trusted me. For the price of those few dollars I spent on that first set of books, he let me trade every week. Except for *Heart of Darkness*. That one I owned and kept with me.

I walked into the warm shop, musty with the smell of old books.

"Annabel," said Lyle from behind the counter, "nice to see you."

I had recently written my name on a slip of paper and handed it to him. Not Ghost, but Annabel. It felt silly to write Ghost. He didn't mention my silence, didn't ask why I never spoke. He accepted it along with my nods and shakes of the head.

Lyle couldn't have weighed more than a hundred and thirty pounds. He wore cardigans that were too big and his fingers stretched out long and skinny like pencils. The shop was always empty. I'd only ever seen one other person in there, and he left without buying anything. To be fair, I went in only once a week and always on the same day, at the same time, but I didn't know how Lyle made money and kept the business going.

"Did you enjoy *The Handmaid's Tale*?" he asked when I gave it back to him.

I nodded.

"Oh good. I thought you would. Maybe you would like to try another?"

I shrugged. Atwood's story both enthralled and disturbed me with its complex characters and their sometimes dangerous choices.

"How about this one?"

On the cover, the profile of a woman's head was divided by horizontal lines into several parts: the profile of the woman on the cover was surrounded by rocky terrain and pine trees, a sun or moon, a figure with a hawk on an outstretched hand, another figure portaging a canoe. Above all that, in calligraphic script: *Surfacing.* Irresistible.

I took it with me. Back at the apartment, I read it in an afternoon.

At first I sympathized with the main character. She had no father figure and yearned for all things paternal that she'd lost. She had grown up poor. She felt awed by nature's forces. I was with her on all that. But, as the book went on, I got angry at her. Here I was sitting in a shit-hole with no family, no home, no education, and no future. I wanted her to shut the hell up and quit bellyaching. That stupid character had it made in the shade compared to me. I wished I had comfortable luxury where I could wallow in self-pity.

Chapter 15

On weekends, Cooper threw parties, big parties with loads of people.

Christmas was mere weeks away and the party people began to turn up in red Santa hats and jingle-bell earrings, with flashing red and green balls pinned to their sweaters.

The drugs, many and varied, made me think of Mama, and I couldn't help feeling sorry for the very high. I wondered if they had families; if they had children at home in bed, kids who needed them.

On a Friday night I sat on a stool beside the couch and watched. I drank enough Purple Jesus — vodka, ginger ale and grape juice — to relax and not worry so much if a stranger tried to talk to me. By now, a lot of the faces looked familiar, even though new people always came and went.

The guy they called Fizzy had hair like steel wool that bounced all around his head while he talked and smoked. He glanced toward me, caught my gaze, and smiled indulgently, like he thought I might be brain damaged or retarded. I crossed my eyes and smiled vacantly back at him. If he wanted to think I was brain damaged, let him.

Francine, whom I had met half a dozen times, wore dark-framed glasses that were so stylish she seemed out of place in our basement hole. I could imagine her cruising the aisles of a fancy store, looking for a designer scarf. Mama always wanted to be that sophisticated woman, in search of beautiful and expensive things. Instead Francine sat on Cooper's filthy couch blowing weed smoke streamers out of her nostrils and working hard at being refined.

It's always best not to try to look *too* cool. Francine sat on that couch looking like ice.

"Butter wouldn't melt in her mouth," Granny would have said. That was the effect Francine thought she achieved. I saw it in her eyes. In truth, her cultivated aloofness was undermined by a bit of green wedged between a couple of her teeth, blinking like an eye through her flapping lips every time she spoke. It might have been spinach or broccoli, and a better person might have gone over and told her. I was not that person. Knowing something about Francine that she didn't know about herself gave me a tiny bit of power I didn't want to give back to her.

Cooper sat on the couch next to her, rolling and bagging joints on the coffee table.

"You and me later, eh?" Cooper said to Francine.

"Fuck you." Francine had a French accent I envied. Even "fuck you" sounded cool and sophisticated.

"You enjoying that shit you're smoking there?" Cooper asked.

"It's mighty fine."

"I paid for it, so you and me later, right?"

"Let's see how the night goes down, *mon amour.*" She stroked the side of his face with her palm, and then slapped, hard. He took hold of her wrist in his big hand and moved his face close to her ear.

"I'll decide how the night goes down, skank. *Oui*?" His lovely white teeth were clenched with malice.

"*Oui. Oui*, I was just kidding."

This little bit of danger went on unnoticed by anyone but me. The room was abuzz with people going about their individual business, everyone with their drunk or drugged-out tunnel vision, caring only about themselves.

I got up and put swift distance between me and the couch, hoping Cooper didn't know I'd overheard. The more of himself he revealed, the more I feared him.

I'd had more to drink than I'd thought and stumbled straight into Graydon. He caught and held me.

"Hey. You okay?"

I nodded.

"A bunch of us are going out later, to a club. I'd really like you to come this time."

I shook my head, backed away, afraid to be accidentally abandoned on the street at night, voiceless and alone.

"I promise to look after you."

I felt the terror in my face, and he must have seen it. "But I won't make you come."

Relieved, I collapsed against his chest and felt him kiss my hair.

"I'll take you out there with me one of these nights, and that's a promise."

Graydon stepped away from me, turned and shrugged on his coat. Cooper stepped between us to grab his boots. When he straightened up, Cooper looked at me with a glare that made my stomach freeze. I tried to appear defiant and stronger than I felt, but he hip-checked me with all his weight and I stumbled against the wall. With so many people milling around the doorway it would have looked like an accident, if anyone had noticed.

Graydon went out with the others, and I went to bed alone with my books.

⌖⌖⌖

I'm walking through a summer field with something warm on my back. Something alive, with breath sweeter than clover puffing against my cheek.

A scent of horses on the breeze makes me stop and take air, in through the nostrils, out through the mouth. I shade my eyes with a hand and spot a dark four-legged figure, framed by sunlight, in the distance. It's moving, getting closer.

The something on my back jumps off and I feel helium-light, like I could fly. I turn and Tully stands behind me, naked except for his glasses. When I turn back, Jett's with us, perfectly groomed, shining and majestic, his old sway back straight as a ruler.

I fall backward into the tall grass. Tully lies beside me; he reaches for me, stroking my belly, thighs, places he has never touched before.

⌖⌖⌖

I awoke with a jolt, disoriented, my hand clamped between my legs. I heard the fridge door open and close.

Cooper and Graydon must have returned home from the bars. I wondered what time it was.

My door was ajar and, through it, I overheard Cooper talking to Graydon, in the fuzzy yet careful way of the very drunk.

"I can't believe that Fran bitch ditched me," said Cooper.

"Aw don't worry about it. You'll catch up with her next time."

"Easy for you to say, man."

152

"What do you mean by that?"

"You got something you won't share. I mean, come on, she can't even cook. She needs to start earning her keep. Now."

"No. She's not ready yet. Give it a little more time."

"You always say 'she's not ready.' That's bullshit. She's perfect. I don't care about ready, man."

I was pretty sure they didn't expect me to earn money at some stupid customer service job or something. I wasn't going to sell sweaters and I couldn't ask anyone if they wanted fries with that.

The thought of Cooper's version of "earning my keep" made me uneasy and I threw the pillow over my head to block out the conversation. But they moved on anyway and started discussing the relative merits of hashish versus marijuana, so I turned over and tried to grab back my dream.

I had a routine and was already bored by it. I dedicated each day to completing something specific. On Monday I went to the Laundromat, Tuesday grocery shopping, Wednesday to visit Lyle at the bookstore, and so on. Not one of those tasks filled an entire day, so I spent the rest of the time taking walks when the weather cooperated, or reading.

Cooper's face had taken on a permanent look of scorn whenever he addressed me. I tried to keep a low profile around the apartment and went off to hide in the mildewed bedroom when he was there.

One Wednesday evening I made a meal but the guys didn't arrive back at the apartment on time so I ate by myself, which was okay with me. I left the food in the pots on the stove for when Graydon and Cooper came in. I didn't know the time, probably around ten or eleven at night, when they finally crashed through the door.

"That fucking guy can stick that shit where the sun don't shine, you know?" said Cooper. He threw his car keys across the room and they landed on the floor behind the couch where I sat. I got up to slink into the bedroom with my book.

"Jesus Christ. This food's fucking cold, and it's shit anyway."

"Cooper, it's, like, eleven o'clock at night. You can't expect the food to still be hot."

"It's my goddamn house, man. I can expect whatever I want. You!" he shouted at me. "You need to be more, um, attentive to my needs."

I stared at him, not sure what I ought to do. An orange flame of rage rose in his brown eyes.

"Gimme that book." He yanked it out of my hands and grabbed the small stack of paperbacks I kept on the floor. He charged into the bathroom and threw them all into the wastebasket. Frantic, I pushed into the bathroom to get my books back.

But Cooper was a solid wall in my way. He took a pack of matches out of his pocket, lit one and dropped it into the can on top of the books. The match fizzled and I seized the opportunity to grab at his arm. He threw me off and I stumbled against the bathtub. He pulled a streamer of toilet paper off the roll, wadded it, and dropped it on top of the books. He tossed in another lit match. This one took. In minutes the books were smoldering and then, with a small whoosh that reminded me of the night the stable went up, the flames started to eat through the books. The pages darkened and curled, and I smelled the chemical scent of the burning binding glue.

By then, I could only stand behind him and watch. I looked at Graydon, who stood with his hands dangling at his sides, as impotent and helpless as I was. When the books had burned beyond retrieval, Cooper walked out and heated the food I'd made.

Cooper was like a hurricane. I never knew when he'd blow in next or what he'd destroy.

I couldn't go back to Lyle without those books. I couldn't explain what had happened. I felt ashamed that I'd allowed the books to be destroyed. And I felt anger. When I went to bed, I lay and breathed through a seething rage at Cooper for what he'd done.

I also wanted to beat against Graydon with my fists for not saving my books from that monster, but I recalled the shred of fear in his eyes when we were crammed together in the doorway of the bathroom.

I stuck my hand under the mattress and felt the worn cover of my copy of *Heart of Darkness*, still whole. At least I had something.

Later, Graydon squeezed into the single bed beside me.

"Cooper's an okay guy, you know. Maybe he has a bit of a temper. But things are going to be fine when I get enough money saved to move out. Then it'll be just you and me, in our own apartment."

I kissed his soft mouth and rolled onto my side. He curved an arm around my waist and slotted his knees behind mine. I thought about Graydon's last sentence, about how it sounded exactly like what Mama used to say.

⊖·⊖·⊖

Warm weather coming in from somewhere else infused the landscape with sallow fog. Black, naked trees grew out of sidewalks. Christmas would have been green at the farm, but downtown it was merely greyish-brown, the colour of the dead mouse I had found under the bed the week before.

I knew it was almost Christmas Day because of the decorations in the mall and the volumes of frenzied people who would kill to put under the tree whatever popular gizmos their kids wanted. But I didn't realize it was actually Christmas morning until Graydon handed me a package wrapped in silver paper.

"Open it," he said, puppy eagerness playing in his face.

I hesitated. I had nothing for him. Why had it not occurred to me to get him something for Christmas?

He had wrapped it himself and the wrapping paper bulged and puckered at the corners. I easily got a finger in the gap and ripped it open. He had taped down the sides of the white oblong box that emerged from the paper, and I struggled to pop through the tape.

"I'll get the scissors."

But by the time he'd handed them to me, I was in. I peered under the pink tissue paper and saw red lace. Graydon had bought me sexy lingerie for Christmas.

I pulled out the red lace thong teddy and stared. He didn't know me at all.

"Put it on."

My head shook "no" before I could stop myself but he looked crestfallen so I changed the shake to a nod. Bundled under my arm, the thing was the size of a hanky. I took it into the bathroom to change.

The garment tag said small and I was medium, at least. My height was in my torso and the thong part felt like it could cut me in half vertically, right up the middle. The coarse lace scratched my skin and embarrassing winter pubic hairs stuck out around the crotch. I tried to stuff them under the lace, but they sprung back out. I felt like a Sasquatch in a red Speedo.

With Cooper gone, Graydon waited for me in the living room. I didn't have much of a choice. There was nowhere to hide. Slouching into myself, my hands clamped in front of me, I shuffled sideways out the bathroom door.

Graydon had eyes only for my body. He didn't seem to notice my discomfort. Before I knew it, the bit of underwear was a puddle of red on the floor beside a hastily opened condom package and Graydon and I were naked across the couch. I felt less self-conscious naked than I had in that red teddy.

⊷⊶⊷

I picked up one of Cooper's ball caps, black with the Ottawa Senators hockey team logo on it, and dropped it into Graydon's lap. When he looked at me, I shrugged and raised my eyebrows.

"Cooper went to his parents' house in Bell's Corners to celebrate Christmas. Yes, he actually has parents."

I curled next to Graydon on the couch and watched the TV screen while he flipped past angelic children singing hymns, a talking cartoon snowman, the Queen — who I felt sorry for because she looked so wretched — until he finally settled on a movie from the seventies that seemed to be about how many cars they could demolish within ninety minutes.

While I watched without interest, I wondered how many family men would throw themselves to the pavement out of twenty-storey windows this season; how many housewives would swing from the rafters by the neck; how many lonely and hopeless people would finally give in to their despair.

I had read somewhere that the suicide rate tripled at Christmastime, but I had never realized such sadness was possible until I sat on that disgusting couch in that horrid apartment with a guy I didn't fully trust. I had no voice, no Granny, no Mama, no Mary and, worst of all, no Tully. It surprised me that no Tully at Christmas felt worse than the lack of anyone else.

"There's no Santa Claus," Granny had said on the first Christmas I spent with her. I'd turned six that year. "So I don't want you to expect any of that claptrap from me."

I'd nodded, but cried afterward, alone in my room. I had wanted the Easter Bunny and the Tooth Fairy — all the illusions Mama gave me — not Granny's sensible reality.

I looked at Graydon's boyish profile. Rather than wallow in misery, I decided to make the best of one of the worst situations of my life. I would make a Christmas dinner. My cooking had improved enough that I'd amassed a small repertoire. I could manage baked chicken, tacos, and spaghetti, as long as I used pre-made frozen meatballs instead of assembling my own.

Chicken was as close as I could come to turkey, so I left Graydon on the couch with his silly film and pulled a package of chicken thighs out of the freezer. I had some frozen corn I could boil and a few potatoes, but when I banged through all the cupboards, I realized I was out of those envelopes of coating for the chicken. I didn't know how to make it any other way. A corner store was sure to be open, even on Christmas Day. A guy named Abdul staffed the one down the block from us. I knew his name only because either his mother or his wife frequently shouted at him from the back room. He shouted back in their language — Arabic, I think.

Abdul and his family were Muslim, so I figured today wouldn't be on their list of holidays that they'd want to close the store for.

I mimed going for a walk. Graydon nodded and turned back to the screen. Each week, Cooper gave me an allotment of money for food. I had got pretty good at budgeting, and managed to feed the three of us on less than he doled out. I had secretly saved fifty dollars already.

I shoved a twenty in my pocket and went out.

The sky was woolly with high grey clouds and the air felt damp. The tiny front yards of the houses were patched with dirty snow and the temperature hovered above zero. The unusual weather made it feel like any early winter day.

Last Christmas, the farm had been a wonderland compared to this, every field covered in smooth whiteness.

The memory smelled like cinnamon and pine. All of us, Char, Tully, Jerome and me, had sat in the kitchen like little kids and decorated the sugar cookies Mary baked. Each of us had a Santa, a tree, and a snowman. Mary set out homemade icing in three colours: red, green and white, and we spread it across the still-warm cookies. We stuck gumdrops into the icing, stealing handfuls of candy from the ceramic bowl and shoving them into our mouths, giggling.

The gifts on Christmas morning had been practical. The stockings held school supplies we had lost or run out of: erasers, pencils, rulers. From under the tree we unwrapped boxes of socks, underwear and sweaters.

At least we had had presents to open, and we had felt safe, almost loved. I hadn't realized how much like family that had been.

By the time I reached the store, dampness had crept into my feet and I stamped them under the tinkling bell. I smiled at Abdul, who sat behind the counter reading a foreign newspaper with wacky symbolic writing. After I got the packets of chicken coating, I stopped to look at the candy display before I went to the counter. A box of Christmas chocolates was already on sale, holiday shopping essentially over. I splurged and bought the chocolates for Graydon. The box had a festive ribbon around it already, as if I'd wrapped it myself.

"Merry Christmas," said Abdul, handing me the bag. His dark face was so friendly I wanted to wish him a Merry Christmas right back, or at least to thank him. All I had was a smile. The good thing about living in a city was that no one expected too much courtesy.

Back in the apartment, Graydon sat where I'd left him.

I pulled the box of chocolates out of the plastic bag and handed it over while I sat down beside him.

"Thanks. Merry Christmas, Baby." He kissed me. "Jesus, you're freezing. I thought it was nice outside."

With his hands, he rubbed warm my fingers and toes, the television images lighting his eyes with other people's fake lives. I closed my eyes and snuggled against him.

"I wish you could talk to me. Tell me how you feel. Maybe someday?"

I didn't have an answer about when, if ever, I'd be able to talk.

We moved apart and he popped a chocolate into my mouth. Sweet cherry goo oozed down my chin and he licked it off. I put another piece between my teeth and teased him with it until he locked his lips over mine and sucked the cherry right out of the chocolate.

He pulled off his clothes and mine, and I went down below to kiss his scars. His lips were on me; I felt them warm and moist.

But his kisses against the shell of my body didn't heal the damage inside. Our kisses were less useful than a Band-Aid on a severed limb. I doubted I healed his damage with my touch any more than he healed mine.

Chapter 16

I muddled through the New Year, pretending it meant nothing to me. Fragmented sounds of night violence invaded my thoughts, images of Granny's dishevelled body lying across the bed.

I believed I'd successfully shed thoughts of Mama, but couldn't help wondering where she might be or what she might be doing. Did she worry about me, even a little? I remembered the panic I felt on September eleventh, when I thought the world might end without me ever seeing her again. Had it really been only three months ago? After all the turmoil, it felt like a decade.

I imagined Mama wandering the streets of Vancouver, the same shambling husk of a human she had been toward the end of Granny's life. If that turned out to be the truth, I didn't ever want to see her again.

Around me now, people snorted, smoked and injected the same kinds of drugs that had ruined Mama's and my life together.

January hit Ottawa hard and cold, making up for the green Christmas with thick ice and mile-high snowdrifts. Graydon, Cooper and I spent more time indoors, coughing phlegm into the air, giving each other colds.

Whenever the guys had a painting contract, or some other odd job, they left early. I liked having the apartment to myself in the morning quiet. I could pretend it was my house, and my husband and children had set off to work and school.

The bedroom was freezing the Monday morning I woke up in the bed alone and remembered Graydon had gone to do some work with Cooper. Before I went out to the bathroom, I picked up a pair of jeans from the bottom of a pile of clothes on the floor and pulled them on. They stopped at my hips and I had to haul hard to get them all the way up. I decided to leave them undone, but when I stood, the hems barely reached the top of my anklebones. These were the jeans I had run in. Christ. I had grown.

When I stepped out into the living room, I saw Francine on the couch, crying. She was wearing only a tight black T-shirt with a blanket across her legs. Vulnerable without her chic glasses, her thin shoulders bucked with near silent sobs.

I wanted to turn around and crawl right back into bed, cover my head with the sheets and hope she'd go away, nothing but a bad hallucination. But the toilet beckoned, so I skirted the couch and went to the bathroom. I tried to take a while — washed my face, brushed my hair, examined my fingernails — but when I came out Francine still sat there sobbing.

I went to her and put my hand on her shoulder. She probably heard me coming because she didn't jump, but she did seem to cry a little harder. I felt bones and muscles moving under her warm skin and cotton shirt.

Nothing changed; she didn't turn to me. Withdrawing the touch I'd offered as a comfort would feel weird, so I was trapped standing beside the couch with my hand on her shoulder.

After several long and awkward minutes, she spoke. "Cooper. He hurt me."

Her statement broke the spell, and I took it as a signal to sit down next to her. What had he done?

She pulled her blanketed knees to her chin, wrapped her arms around her shins and rocked like an autistic child. If Cooper had hurt her during the night, in the room next to mine, I hadn't heard a thing. I hooked my finger into a strand of her loose hair and tucked it behind her ear. She looked up at me. Her mouth had a rash around it, a perfect red rectangle. Cooper had taped her silent, the bastard.

"I got pregnant," she said. "When I told him, last night, Cooper got so mad, wild, you know?"

I knew. I could picture Cooper's face in a maniacal rage, like when he hip-checked me into the wall or burned my books, only worse. Terrifying.

"He used things on me. In me."

Not quite getting what she was telling me, I waited for her to go on.

"He took the baby out using...well...things." Francine's fingers trembled and her mouth formed a small O of shock and fear. "I kept bleeding, all over everything, and he got madder."

Sweet Jesus. She covered her face with her hands and sobbed silently into her palms.

I got up and went to Cooper's room where I found a pile of white sheets soaked with bright red blood. I came out to the couch and pulled her to standing and watched her face turn paler, caught her as she swooned. The blanket under her bottom was red, and a rusty smudge had seeped onto the cushion.

"I'm so tired." Francine flopped back to the couch.

Hospital. I had to get her to the hospital or she was going to die right there in front of me. Cooper had taken his car. If I called 911 they would find me. I was a runaway from a foster home, and the cops would probably want to search the place, ask questions I couldn't answer, nose around into all my business. I'd be in even more trouble.

I breathed and willed my hands to stop shaking. Francine's life depended on me not freaking out. I felt suddenly too hot to think straight. When I stepped out the front door and stood on the frozen concrete in my bare feet, it came to me: we could take the city bus.

Back inside, I stripped Francine and sat her in a tub of warm water to wash away the crusty blood. Rather than look at her, I focused on the blood that swirled down the drain.

I left her in the tub and got a clean pair of my own underwear and stuffed it with three thick maxi-pads for Francine. After I got dressed, I slammed the yellow pages onto the kitchen counter and flipped through it until I found a list of hospitals. I had to cross-reference that with maps in the front to find the nearest one. I had to look at the ceiling and breathe a bunch of times so that panic wouldn't whisk me away. I ripped the page with the map on it right out of the phone book to take with me.

After I got some clothes on, I helped Francine get dressed, and then I practically carried her out the door to the bus stop. She was a smaller person than I expected. She had seemed much larger when I watched her snobby face at those parties, ignoring me like I was vermin. I thought of the bit of green between her teeth and how I hadn't told her about it.

At the bus stop she closed her eyes and rested her head on my shoulder. "I'm so cold," she said.

She was clothed in everything I could find. All her outdoor wear and some of mine, including my gloves. My hands were freezing in my pockets.

I looked at the map on the inside of the bus shelter wall and held the one from the phone book up next to it. I noted the route and bus numbers we needed to take to get to the closest hospital. We were lucky; it was only two buses.

The bus stopped in front of us, air brakes hissing in the cold. I helped her up the steps and clinked the change into the receptacle. The bus warmed me and I felt surer of myself. I could do this.

The wait for the next bus was longer. I listened to Francine's soft moans and worried she'd start bleeding through the pads and underwear and give us away before we got to the emergency room.

When the bus arrived and we got off the bench, I looked back at the seat but didn't see blood. Maybe she would heal and be okay after all.

A man in a long wool coat and a woman with high-heeled black boots stared at us but I ignored them. No one ever *did* anything in the city. They only stared. I pulled Francine closer and buried my mouth in her hair, like we were lesbian lovers. They looked away.

Our stop approached and I had a crazy fantasy of shoving Francine out onto the sidewalk in front of the hospital and letting the bus take me away.

Instead, we hobbled out the back door of the bus and walked down an icy path toward the Emergency Room entrance, past hastily parked ambulances and hospital personnel who smoked cigarettes in the cold.

After walking through the sliding glass doors we were enveloped in the warmth of festering germs and the green stink of disinfectant. When I felt Francine collapse against me in a convenient final swoon, I let her fall gently to the floor. I had made sure her wallet was in her coat pocket. They would find it and know who she was. If she had family, the hospital would find them too. I didn't know how old she was because I didn't bother to pry into the ID in her wallet, but I guessed not more than twenty.

I turned to leave and heard, "Hey," from someone behind me. I kept walking. Francine's prone body must have provided a good distraction because, although I expected a firm hand on my shoulder at any second, none came.

⟶⟵⟶⟵⟶⟵

I waited at the bus stop while cold bit at my fingers. I'd left my only pair of gloves on Francine's hands. A bus plastered with the smiling faces of local radio hosts carried me to the empty apartment, which I refused to think of as home.

I scrubbed the stain on the couch with a J-cloth until it turned beige and blended with all the other stains. And then I sat beside it, listening to the room's small sounds. The fridge rumbled; the baseboard heaters ticked off and on. Francine's bloodless face bobbed in and out of my mind, her skin like paper, and her eyelids closed and bluish. I hoped she would live. Maybe the hospital would find her parents and they would arrive at the hospital before it was too late. They would hover over her with worried faces, apology in their eyes. Her mother would cry and take her home, tuck her into bed, kiss her forehead. I wondered if I would ever find out what happened to Francine. Sometimes people come and go, like the way Jerome did.

I didn't touch the pile of bloody sheets in the corner of Cooper's room. When I was scrubbing the bathtub with a squirt of Vim with bleach, I saw a black shape in the bathroom wastebasket, the remains of something burned and unrecognizable. It might have been a bunch of twigs. When I poked at it with a drinking straw the little pile disintegrated into ash. I dumped the ashes into the kitchen garbage and rinsed out the wastebasket with its black scorch marks from the books that Cooper burned the week before.

Sometime after that, the early January twilight turned the prison-like windows from grey to black and Graydon and Cooper stamped through the door. They sniffed and sighed while pulling off boots, coats and hats, the smell of cold snow clinging to their clothes and hair.

The lights came on.

"Ghost? What are you doing sitting in the dark?" Graydon asked. "You okay?"

"Why do you even bother asking her questions?" Cooper shot me a mean smile and his teeth looked like tombstones, smooth and ready for engraving. "I mean she's actually the perfect woman. Not only can she not answer, she can't talk back or ask you where you been, who you been with, when you're coming back. She can't even tell anyone else what you been up to. That's my idea of perfect, man." He pulled his back straight, looking impossibly tall, a smug gleam in one eye.

I wished I could put my fist straight into the socket until that eyeball popped out the back of his round skull. Cooper went to the kitchen and opened and closed the cold oven.

"Aw, shit. She didn't even make anything for us to eat."

"That's okay, Coop," said Graydon, looking at me with eyes as round as a baby's. "I feel like pizza anyway. I'll buy." He picked up the phone and called for pizza.

While Graydon was in the shower, I watched Cooper wander around the apartment, trying to figure out what to do about the mess in the corner of his room, but pretending he wasn't. In the end, he got a yellow plastic garbage bag from the kitchen and disappeared behind the bedroom door.

The next day, the bag was on the curb with the rest of the garbage, the contents so anonymous it might have contained anything, even the whole of Francine's little body.

⌘

During the time I'd spent in the dark, between dropping Francine off at the hospital and Graydon and Cooper coming home, I imagined pulling myself inward. I pictured drawing my legs and arms, right from the tips of my fingers and toes, into the core of me, for strength. It was the only way I could stay in that apartment and survive. The idea of leaving, running Out There alone, I kept as a kernel of terror somewhere in the middle of my brain.

I emerged from the darkness harder on the outside, with the soft parts smaller, buried. And my silence felt deeper than ever.

Chapter 17

"C'mon, Baby. Let me show you off. It'll be fun."
It was Saturday night and Graydon pressed his forehead against mine, his hands clasped behind my buttocks. I figured he felt badly that I always stayed alone at the apartment while he went out. He probably pictured me crying into my pillow, a heartsick, lonely teenager. Truth was I preferred evening solitude to a crowd. Being surrounded by tons of people confused me, made me feel lonelier than ever.

"I won't leave you by yourself for a minute. I even promise to take you into the men's room with me." He grinned and made a Scouts' honour sign.

This was the millionth time he'd asked me. His plot to wear me down through nagging was working. Since I'd managed to get Francine to the hospital on the bus, I felt less afraid of the city and more reckless. I'd been Out There alone and survived, and I was starting to feel like I had less to lose.

I nodded. He whooped quietly. "You won't regret it. We'll have a blast."

When we stepped out the door after the others — there were about ten of us that night — he held his arm out like a gentleman and I hooked my elbow into his. Part of me felt like a film star, part like a teenage runaway, part a kind of numbness, like it was all happening to someone else.

We walked along the sidewalk. Pebbles and bits of gravel were frozen to the surface of the concrete. The Dominion Tavern on the Market was one of several places that didn't bother to card under-aged kids, which made it ideal for us. Cooper was legal — I think he was somewhere in his twenties — and some of the others had IDs too. But the Canadian government definitely considered Graydon and me too young to drink. Funny, because sometimes I felt so old I could hear my dusty bones rattle around inside me, and sometimes I felt like a sad child who had dropped her ice cream cone upside down on a dirty floor.

The Dom had a narrow frontage to the street and stretched back toward a couple of filthy washrooms. Inside, the whole place was so thin and long they could barely squeeze in a couple of ripped green-felt pool tables. And people had to stand all the way against the opposite wall to get distance from the dartboards. Walking to the washrooms was like crawling across No Man's Land.

Cooper went straight to the bar and ordered six pitchers. We spread ourselves out over three sticky tables, and a couple of the guys bought a pool game and took off to play. Graydon stayed on my right, like he promised he would. I rested my head on his shoulder, feeling his muscles shift against my cheek as he talked.

When Cooper got restless, we moved on.

"He never stays at one place longer than an hour," Graydon said with his beer breath as we walked out. "Unless there's a cover charge. If there's a cover, he'll stay for two hours." We went out into the frigid night air. I shivered and he put his arm around my shoulders.

We walked past a group of three hookers, smoking and talking on the sidewalk. One of them stepped toward us, and Cooper, who was in the lead, began to wave her away, dismissing her anonymous whore-ness.

I glanced at her face. It was Charlene.

She looked terrible. Cheeks so hollow they could hide a mouse, and eyes like fathomless black pits. Her makeup stood out as if it were painted on cellophane and held up in front of her face. Her legs were far apart and skinny, disappearing separately up a skirt that barely covered her bottom. My mother's legs. Her vacant eyes sunk into her gaunt face. My mother's eyes. Char was addicted.

"Ghost, you bitch!" she shrieked when she recognized me. She lunged at me with bright red claws. I deked out of her way, but she caught the back of my coat and pulled me toward her. I struggled.

"You fucked up everything. I'll kill you!"

She scratched and punched at my face with her free hand. I tried to grab her wrist, but her hand whipped around like the frantic end of a high-pressure hose. Somehow she managed to kick at my shins at the same time.

I stopped trying to defend myself and wrapped my arms around my head. I struggled to undo her grip on my coat by spinning in circles and then I felt her let go and the blows stopped raining on me.

When I took my arms from my face, Graydon had Char in a wrestling hold I couldn't remember the name of. A half-something. I heard his voice rasp into Char's ear. "You better get outta here or we'll call the cops."

She gave me a murderous look.

"You got that?" Graydon asked, sending a tremor through her body by shaking her. "I'm not letting you go until you agree to get the hell out of here."

She nodded. The two other hookers had gathered closer to us and they exchanged profanity with Cooper at the top of their voices. Char's mascara had run into black half-moons that stained the skin under her eyes, making the rest of her pale face stark and ghostly. Graydon let her go and she threw her hands up in a posture of surrender. Without taking her gaze from mine, she picked up the little sequined handbag she had dropped and swung it over one shoulder. With the other hand, she pointed at me and smiled in a sinister grimace that made my hands sweat despite the cold. My knees felt weak.

The hookers pulled her along with them, and we went the opposite way, toward the Dominion again. Now that my back was to her, I imagined her red-claw fingers digging into my shoulder, pulling me back. I shuddered.

I heard Cooper laugh. "That was a great show, but what the hell was it all about?"

"Shut up, Cooper," said Graydon.

"Hey, man, I was only asking."

"Just someone we used to know, okay?"

Why was Char back on the street? Had she run too, or had something terrible happened after the barn burned down? She said I'd fucked up everything, but I didn't know what that meant.

I thought of Tully, how vulnerable he had always been and how frightened. If Char was not with Mary and Bobby anymore, maybe Tully wasn't either. I hoped he'd found a decent foster family to live with.

I thought of Tully's smooth voice reading out passages from his books, his small hand in mine during a rainstorm, his soft breath while he lay in the bed beside me.

At that moment, I would have traded Graydon's embrace for Tully's in a heartbeat.

◦⊶⊷◦

I had a single long scratch down each side of my face, almost exactly parallel, from cheek to chin. Blood had already begun to harden in the scratches by the time I was safe in the bathroom, looking into the mirror, hardly believing what I saw there. My right eye was swelling and turning black. I dabbed at the scratches with a wet cloth, my hand trembling. The thin wounds stung.

I wished I'd fought harder. I wished Graydon had rescued me quicker. It was like being twelve all over again, when I got beaten up at the mall by those rich girls. I wondered if I was destined to be a victim forever. I thought about the time Patrick got stuffed up the brick chimney. I thought about the scars Graydon's father had left on him. I thought about how Tully's parents rejected him before they even got to know him. Maybe everyone was just a victim.

I went to the couch and sat next to Graydon. He traced the scratches with his thumb. His face looked unusual, pale and decorated with some kind of fear or worry, the face of a small boy lost in the woods. I had put my life, my fate, in the hands of this child. My fingers trembled harder when I looked at him, so I pressed them tightly over my eyes. I felt him shifting around on the couch.

"Hey," he said, and I peeked out. He took one of my hands, pulled it toward him and dropped a small white pill from his palm into mine. "Take this. It'll help you sleep." He put one

173

into his own mouth and I watched his Adam's apple rise and fall with his swallow.

I looked into my palm. Cupped in its soft pink lines was the tiny pill. I popped it into my mouth and swallowed it before Graydon handed me a glass. I drank the water anyway, my dry mouth grateful. I went to the bedroom and lay on the bed.

A feeling of profound loss floated me toward the ceiling where I found Tully and Jett in our field of wildflowers.

I knelt to take Tully in my arms, pure joy, when blackness filled me up and shut me down.

Grey days followed. The pill I had taken made me afraid of becoming my mother. Even though I hadn't asked for it, I had taken it, innocent and white, from Graydon's hand. Only because I'd been shaken when that crazy Charlene attacked me on the sidewalk with her bare hands. I had wanted to push her wild painted face out of my head so I could sleep and forget. Her mad eyes, black-and-red rimmed, so angry, flashed a pain through my skull at any time of the day or night. I could be standing and staring into the refrigerator, having forgotten why I opened it. I could be walking down Rideau Street in broad daylight. I could be asleep in bed next to Graydon.

Now, when I looked at Graydon, I saw the pale fear, which he wore like a pair of familiar jeans. I realized he had begun to cling to me now, the way I had clung to him at Noble Spirit. I think he was afraid of living in that ratty apartment with Cooper, but also afraid of getting kicked out. Afraid of foraging for food and warmth on bare winter streets. It seemed like the two of us against Cooper and the rest of the city. Graydon depended on Cooper for work, food and shelter and on me for comfort and guidance, but all I wanted was a mama. Not my mama, necessarily, but someone like Mary, who would put her hands on me, maybe even rock me, and tell me everything was going to be all right.

But there was only me, and the little boy that Graydon had become.

◦◦◦◦◦

Out of necessity, I was acquiring new skills. I had learned how to grocery shop once a week without getting so much of something that it spoiled before I used it up or too little of something else that it ran out early. I could cook so that we didn't have to throw quite so many spoiled food combinations into the garbage. And I had even grown to enjoy the steamy quiet of the Laundromat on a Monday afternoon. The edges of my book curled and the pages were warped, accordion-like, with moisture.

The Friday night that my time with Graydon ended seemed typical, except I caught Cooper looking at me a lot. Sideways looks. The ones where his head stayed straight ahead, but his eyes slid over to stare at me, an expression on his face like he'd been struck by the smirk-fairy. His gaze made me want to cover myself in a big sack so he couldn't see any part of me. I never hated anyone like I hated Cooper.

Graydon didn't know what was going to happen that night. When I look back on it, I'm sure he had no idea. But I don't know what he would have done about it anyway.

It was a punch party. A huge stainless steel bowl filled with dark red drink sat on the kitchen counter like a bowl of blood. Another bowl with purple punch slopping around in it was on the coffee table. In a plastic bucket on the floor someone had mixed the rest of both together, which created a liquid that was an unpleasant shade of brown, reminding me of very loose diarrhea.

I watched while a moderately drunk Fizzy attempted to get a clip onto a roach. His tongue between his teeth, he gave it several game and earnest tries before he nudged the guy next to him for help.

A hand settled on my shoulder and I looked into Cooper's face.

"Truce?" he said, and held out a white plastic beer cup half-full of bloody punch. I took it because I wanted it, not because I would agree to any truce with Cooper. I lived in his house and ate his food, but I wished every minute that Graydon and I had enough saved to get a place of our own, away from Cooper.

The punch tasted Kool-Aid sweet and the outside of the cup made my fingers sticky. Heady and strong with rum, I felt it after my first gulp. The cottony sensation in my head was nice, emotionless. I drank more.

The beat of rap music quivered through my chest. Fizzy and a girl I hadn't seen before flailed across the floor in an approximation of a dance, Fizzy's cigarette hanging off his bottom lip, his hair a wild creature trying to escape from his head. I laughed at the thought, my laugh emerging an unnatural, tinny sound.

My face had gone numb. I watched my hand lose its grip on the plastic cup, which clacked onto the linoleum, the last of my drink spilling out across the floor. An urge for fresh air made me stand up. I fell sideways. I hadn't realized I was falling until Cooper's arms were around me, hoisting my weight onto his hip and shoulder.

"Whoa. Someone's had a bit too much. I'm putting Ghost to bed," he announced to the room.

I didn't see if anyone was listening to Cooper because I couldn't hold my head up. The linoleum floor tiles, sticky with purple, red and brown splotches, and filthy with boot marks, whizzed by me as Cooper carried me to the bedroom.

He dropped me on the bed and, despite my feeble protests, pulled off my jeans and socks. He leaned over me, smoothed the hair out of my face, and said, "Sleep tight, Little Ghost." He turned off the light, but didn't cover me up.

I struggled and fumbled until I had a blanket over my feet and legs, and then I gave up and lay back, my ears buzzing, head spinning. What was going on? I'd only had one cup of the punch, plus a beer or two earlier in the evening. It didn't make sense. The turmoil of confusion in my head didn't let me sleep, so I lay in the dark, unable to move.

The light flipped on and music spilled into the room. The door shut again and the sound of boot thumps echoed against the yellow-stained walls. The edge of the bed sagged with a weight.

"Let's try you out, shall we?" Cooper's whisper came hot and moist beside my ear. The room's atmosphere filled instantly with electricity and tension. I pushed my eyelids as open as I could, which wasn't more than a slit. I saw only the side of Cooper's head, the shadowed swirl of one ear.

The tinkle of a belt buckle made a sweaty scream of fear push against my forehead. All I managed was a gurgling sound.

The drug had removed some of the terror and replaced it with numbness, a paralysis of the body that, in a twist of cruelty, had not taken my mind with it. If only I could have passed into unconsciousness so memory would be softened and veiled, or disappear entirely. Male sweat, rank beer and soft grunting stuffed my nose, mouth and ears. I felt no pain, but knew the violation Cooper committed. He was rough, savage even.

I tried to think of nothing, but couldn't. So I filled my head with memories and imaginings that I hoped might soothe. I tried to let Mary pull me into her huge bosom, but Cooper gave off a faint whiff of talcum powder, like Mary's, which destroyed any sanctuary that illusion might provide.

Instead I let Tully lie down beside me in the bed, his bony forehead against my cheek. Then Jett was on my other side, blowing velvet-soft, apple-scented breath onto my shoulder. I pictured Jerome's face by the firelight, telling his Native fire story about the strength of tiny Grandmother Spider, how she never gave up.

These creatures, human and animal, which formed the best of my recent memories, pulled me along, from first thrust to last. And I felt so grateful that I wept through my half-closed eyelids, tears pooling in the hollows of my ears.

"What the fuck's going on?" Graydon screamed.

Cooper rolled off and the belt buckle tinkled again, more frantically, it seemed, than it had the first time.

"What do you think's going on, man? I told you I wasn't gonna wait around anymore for your approval."

"What did you do to her?"

I expected Graydon to come to me, hold me. I saw him through the slits in my eyelids. But he stood by the door, a look of terror in his wide-open stare.

"What do you think, asshole? I was sampling the goods. Next time it'll be one of the customers in here with her, and we'll get some actual cash. You owe me, man. *She* owes me."

⊷⊷⊷

In the morning, I pressed my thighs hard together, hoping to heal myself by sealing the opening closed forever. Like I had seen Francine try to do while she almost bled to death on the couch.

I felt bruised and as delicate as a moth's wing. My skin might rip open at the slightest movement. In the night, Graydon had cried into my ear.

"Cooper told me you went to bed early. I didn't know. I didn't know."

When I could move again, I turned my back to him. He spooned me tightly, weeping until the fine hairs on the back of my neck were wet with his tears.

"I thought I could hold him off until we got a place of our own. Cooper promised he'd wait. I didn't know he'd decided on tonight. He's like a brother to me. We grew up together and he looked after me. Oh God. He's right. I do owe him. My mom died when I was only ten years old. After that, my dad got real bad with the drinking and using me like an ashtray and punching bag, so Cooper's family let me stay with them. They fed me and made sure I had clean clothes to wear. When I got in shit at school with the other kids, Cooper beat the crap out of them for me."

I pictured Cooper, big and mean like now, picking up little kids two at a time, one in each hand, and tossing them aside. Little third graders lying on the sidewalk, crumpled dead like road kill, while Cooper stepped over them, Graydon held above his head like a prize. Did Graydon really think he owed Cooper that much? That he owed him me?

Right then, I hated them both. I had blacked out, finally.

⟨∘⟩⟨∘⟩⟨∘⟩

I awoke in the early light that turned the room, and everything in it, bluish-grey and indistinct. A throbbing ache rose through my pelvis. I felt dirtier than if I'd rolled naked in swamp mud and then coated myself in sand. I felt dirty from the inside out.

I left Graydon in bed and hobbled to the bathroom, using the sheet to hold myself together. I thought my insides might come whooshing right out onto the floor. I sat on the cold toilet seat and peed. Miraculously, my kidneys and liver didn't leave my body, but I saw a few thin strands of blood swaying in the toilet water when I stood up.

Water splashed into the bathtub after I turned on the tap, and the sound made me need to pee again. This time peeing stung but only urine the colour of pale straw came out.

The bathwater was so hot that wraiths of steam rose in fading ribbons into the cold bathroom air. I stepped into the tub and my foot went immediately red up to the waterline on my ankle. I breathed through my teeth and got my whole body into that searing water. With a bar of soap and a washcloth I scrubbed every inch of puckered, red skin.

I curled up in a corner of the tub and cried and cried until I was done, salty tears joining the ocean around me. I lay up to my neck in water and figured out some things, and made some decisions for myself.

With a clarity that emerged out of the fog of pain low in my belly I contemplated how I had been lured here. How Graydon and Cooper had worked it all out between them.

I had finally earned my keep, like a hooker. Like Charlene. I didn't understand how Graydon could sell me like that. I hadn't appreciated Mary and Bobby G, and had wasted my energy pining away for a mama who didn't want me, but this punishment for my selfishness seemed pretty extreme.

I'd wasted months of my life in servitude to Cooper. I thought I was helping to make a home for me and Graydon, even if it was temporarily under someone else's roof.

Graydon regretted bringing me here, I knew that. He thought he could hold Cooper off forever, but he lost more power every day. Any power he thought he had over Cooper was an illusion anyway. I could see that now. Cooper was, and had always been, in total control. He was a hell of a clever guy.

The bath water went cool. Goosebumps stood out all over my skin when I toweled off, the vigorous scrubbing still not quite getting rid of the filthy feeling.

I stepped onto the ragged dishcloth that Cooper used as a bathmat and shook my head. Droplets of water shot off the ends of my hair and stuck to the steamy mirror, reflecting the bathroom light. Shaking my head made me feel nauseated and trembly. My stomach took a sudden lurch and I vomited into the toilet.

I brushed my teeth to get rid of the sour smell, and then I brushed them again.

I didn't know what waited for me Out There, but Out There was the only choice I had left.

Chapter 18

After I got dressed I went into the closet in the bedroom that Graydon and I shared. Cooper stored a bunch of stuff in there, including a few empty travel bags. I figured the bastard owed me more than a lousy canvas backpack, but that was all I took. I wanted nothing else from him anyway, except my freedom. I grabbed the pack and shoved in all my clothes, including the dirty stuff. I slung the straps around my shoulders to keep my hands free.

Graydon was still sleeping. I considered leaning over and giving him a strong slap across the cheek but I dreaded waking him and facing a confrontation. Instead I grabbed his grey hooded sweatshirt and pulled it over my head. It smelled like him and so I took that too.

With almost eighty dollars and the bag of clothes, I bolted out alone into the frigid early Ottawa morning.

The streets were freezing. A few weeks ago I'd replaced the gloves I left on Francine's hands, but I had cheaped out and the new gloves were too thin. My toque was equally inadequate, so I pulled the hood of the sweatshirt out of the neck of my jacket and up over my head. The chill air went straight through it anyway.

This running away thing was shaping up to be a bad idea. But I didn't have a choice. I couldn't stay in that apartment a single second longer.

I walked along the sidewalk, turning left or right on nothing more than whim, keeping the thin sunlight of a winter morning at my back. The cold air smelled of coffee and breakfast, and my stomach tumbled. I had to be careful with my money because I didn't know how long it would be before I could acquire more. Or how I might go about acquiring it. Without a Social Insurance Number, a voice, or a place to shower, I wasn't exactly over-qualified to get a job. I'd never even had a job before.

I reasoned that breakfast was the cheapest meal of the day. You got a lot for a little, if you went to the right place. I chose a diner that looked clean but cheap, and sat at a table in the back corner where I ordered scrambled eggs, bacon and toast by pointing at food items on the sticky plastic menu. I sipped hot, scorched coffee and enjoyed the warmth. I'd never sat alone at a restaurant.

There would be a lot of firsts on my first truly homeless day.

The mall downtown seemed as good a place as any to hang out and stay warm. It was big and busy and anonymous. I'd been gone from Mary's for so long I hoped by now the child welfare authorities had stopped looking for me. And I knew Cooper hated shopping so it felt less likely I'd run into him there. I carried an image of Cooper in my mind that would later haunt my dreams, his face purple with rage, pursuing me through dark alleys and winding streets, his fingers almost touching the back of my neck.

By midday, the mall was crowded. Government bureaucrats in uniform dark suits and bright silk ties lined up at fast food counters and ate hamburgers out of paper wrappers at tables that were bolted to the floor. They sipped Evian water and talked and laughed while their ID cards swayed on chains around their necks.

I fished a newspaper out of a trashcan. Perched on a bench, I read it slowly, peering over the top to watch people with real lives bustle past on their way somewhere more important than here.

"Excuse me."

Bewildered, I looked up from my paper, not really believing anyone could be talking to me. A guy in a brown uniform stood beside the bench. He had a patchy moustache and spotty skin.

"You can't sit here. There's a bylaw against loitering, you know. You have to move along." He demonstrated his point by waving his arm in circles like an overzealous traffic cop. "Come on now. Move along."

How did he know I wasn't waiting for someone? He must have had some kind of mall cop homeless teenager radar, an over-developed sense of anti-loitering duty.

I bundled the paper under my arm and walked off toward the main escalators. I wasn't prepared to go back outside into the cold, so I wandered instead; going into shops and fingering stuff I had no intention of buying, to kill time.

In every store the clerks hustled to the front when they saw me walk in, and followed me through the racks until I left. I made a game of it. I counted the seconds to see how long it would take for one of them to notice I'd come in and start tailing me. Two minutes and ten seconds was the longest, thirty-seven seconds the shortest.

The mall, huge and complicated, had hallways that intersected and then went off in eccentric directions. It was as if no one had properly planned it. I got lost a couple of times and popped outside onto streets I didn't recognize.

I found a pedestrian catwalk that connected one part of the mall to the part that was on the other side of the street. Halfway across, I stopped and looked out at the cars and buses that travelled below my feet, greyish-white exhaust pluming from car undercarriages into the frigid air. Sidewalk people rushed from doorway to doorway in the cold, holding their coats tight around their bodies.

Four girls walked past me, giggling and snapping at bubblegum. I snatched a piece of their conversation.

"I finished my driver's ed. I'm taking the written test next month, and then my dad says he'll take me out in the Volvo anytime I want. You know, to practice."

By the end of next summer I would be old enough to take my driver's test. Those girls who swept past me with their carefree long hair and fashionable clothes were the same age as I was.

My heart was seized by a loneliness so overwhelming I almost crumpled into a heap to the floor of the catwalk, but I kept on walking to the other side of the mall, not wanting to risk loitering. Not wanting to get "moved along" once again.

Until the end of the day, my mission was clear: keep moving and avoid mall cops at all costs. Lone teenagers were apparently easy to spot and toss out into the street.

In the public washroom, I checked the bruised area between my legs, which had begun to throb with so much walking. My skin would heal.

Late afternoon, I watched the food court closely. A mother struggled with her two kids, trying to get them to eat their fast food meal. One kid cried and wailed and downright refused to eat. The mother gave in, like I knew she would. She looked as if she'd spent all day getting pulled back and forth like a rope in a tug-of-war. She got up from the table and dragged the kids away behind her, too preoccupied to bother dumping the uneaten food in the trash.

The food court was loud and busy and no one noticed when I sat down at the table and claimed the leftover food as my own. By that time I was starving and I stuffed that kid's barely touched hamburger into my mouth. It was cold but good. I hoped that boy wasn't suffering from any kind of sickness picked up from his snot-filled kindergarten class. The older kid had left two batter-covered, greasy chicken nuggets. I ate those too.

I sensed the darkness before I was out in it. Skylights had gone black and even indoors had a feeling of night. Short winter days meant darkness fell way before the mall closed.

When the mall was almost empty except for the guards, I left through an unfamiliar door and didn't know which direction to go. The Byward Market streets at night were brighter than the streets around the apartment. The weather had warmed enough that snow drifted down in fat white chunks, like slow motion rain, through orange streetlamp glow.

My legs were rubbery with the exhaustion of carrying my weight in circles for the past eight hours. My loose pants chafed at my injuries. But out here, as inside the mall, it seemed important to keep moving.

I got hit by the rank urine stink of alleyways as I trucked past them, head down, walking with a purpose I didn't have. It was a smell so strong even the coldness of the air couldn't hold it at bay. A bum squatted in a doorway. He'd fallen asleep with his filthy hand out, resting on a grubby bent knee, his palm clad in a ragged, fingerless brown glove.

The shambling drunks didn't scare me much. They were so hopeless I figured I could outrun them without trying. It was the kids who made my heart pound in fear. Wiry kids wearing backward baseball caps travelled in packs like wolves, foamy dots of spittle freezing onto the sidewalk around them. Their bodies emitted desperation and electric violence. Through the swirling snow, I spotted a group of them, the obvious leader giving the rest of them ideas. He wore big black boots that looked super warm, and baggy black pants with white stitching, the crotch webbed between his knees.

I crossed the street to avoid them. If I pretended I had somewhere to go — that someone was waiting for me in a warm house — they'd leave me alone. I hoped. I didn't want to be the mouse to their cat.

When I hit the next corner, I realized with some relief that I knew where I was. I had managed to walk all the way around the mall until I came upon the familiar entrance.

In a few more blocks, I'd be at my destination. What I would do when I got there depended on what I found. I was winging it, but didn't figure I had much to lose.

I slowed when I walked past the Dominion Tavern. Someone opened the door to go in, and warm air seeped out. In front of me stretched nothing but empty sidewalk. I trudged on, to the spot where I'd seen her last, but there were no painted ladies in doorway shadows, least of all the one I was interested in.

I had no plan, only the hope that if I ran into Char, she wouldn't kill me, but would tell me what had happened to her, and the farm, after we ran away. I didn't know how I was going to get her to talk to me without using her fists. With no voice, my powers of persuasion were pretty limited. I wished Graydon had asked her all those questions when we saw her that first time. If she hadn't been so angry, so violent, we might have considered sitting down with her for a drink someplace, talking like the old friends we should have been. Char probably hated me for running off with Graydon. She thought she had him all to herself, and maybe had even painted rosy pictures in her head of them getting married and living happily ever after.

But Char's absence spared me, at least for the moment. There were no hookers around at all. Maybe I was too early. It couldn't have been later than about ten or eleven o'clock. The human traffic to bars along that strip of the Market was only beginning. Or maybe this wasn't her regular spot. She and her companions might have been on their way to somewhere else when she'd spotted me and Graydon. I glanced nervously behind me, worried Graydon or Cooper might be out there looking for me. If Cooper caught up with me, I planned to raise a huge stink. I'd rather get caught by the cops than go anywhere with him.

To get out of the snow, I leaned my back against the recessed wall of a doorway. It led to some kind of eclectic shop full of new but mostly useless junk, like bamboo wind chimes and smooth bowls carved out of exotic brown wood. The shop had closed for the night, but a light still glimmered inside to illuminate the goods and discourage thieves, but I had to figure thieves had better things to steal.

Cigarette packages and other bits of paper were frozen to the sidewalk, blown into the doorway by bitter wind and trapped in its pocket of dead air.

I swung my backpack off my shoulder, unzipped the front pouch, and rummaged around for the pen and pad of paper I'd brought with me. I sat on the cold concrete and nestled my back into the corner between glass and brick while I thought about what I wanted to write. The note needed to mess things up for

Cooper. It had to be compelling enough to incite action. Some exaggeration was in order.

After a few false starts, which I crumpled and stuffed back into my bag, I felt I had written a pretty good note. The place I needed to go was too far for tonight. I would figure out the route and splurge by taking the bus in the morning. My legs ached and I felt light-headed, like a fever was beginning to bloom. I needed rest but didn't know where to go so I stayed put and watched the snow fall.

From where I sat, I could see the Chateau Laurier, floodlights shining in wedges of yellow light across the walls. Beyond that, unseen, the Rideau Canal and the Parliament buildings. I had taken a class tour of downtown Ottawa in elementary school. At the time, it had seemed remote, even while I stood right beside the Eternal Flame on the grounds in front of the Centre Block building. Even then I knew that this city belonged to other people, not to me.

Ottawa was a government town. It used to piss Granny off when people referred to the government as "Ottawa." The news anchors always did it: "And Ottawa, today, passed legislation to limit special education in public schools." Or whatever ridiculous thing the government was trying to do. Granny defended her city whenever she heard stuff like that.

"What do they mean 'Ottawa'? Ottawa doesn't make decisions or pass legislation. It's those dunder-headed politicians on Parliament Hill who screw up Canada, not the City of Ottawa."

I agreed with her. Ottawa wasn't only the government. From my vantage point on the street, it was a whole lot more. Ottawa was both rich and poor. If you belonged to one group, you didn't belong to the other. Poverty and homelessness ran afoul of Mercedes Benzes and Holt Renfrew. Ottawa was

Rockcliffe Park with multi-million-dollar embassies, and the Men's Mission and the Salvation Army. It had restaurants that sold thirty-dollar entrees and bridge overpasses that sheltered the homeless. It was dichotomy and hypocrisy. It was a city that suffered the same problems as any other city.

I remembered a movie I'd watched with Graydon late one night on television. The characters stood on top of a skyscraper in an anonymous downtown and exclaimed about the beauty of the cityscape that stretched before them. I looked out of my doorway at the grey street, bleak stone buildings and somber steel-framed glass windows. I thought of the alleyways that held the stench of garbage and human waste. I couldn't reconcile the idea of beauty with the ugliness of what I saw. Give me field or forest any day. Television was full of lies.

Ottawa at night, however, wasn't quite as sinister as I'd imagined it would be. There was a kind of changing of the guard going on. Beautiful people, men in long wool coats and silk scarves, women in fur, were leaving the swanky restaurants and heading for their luxury cars and SUVs. Young people — buzzed on store-bought beer and wearing cheap shoes — were on their way to the nightclubs.

No one glanced at me, out here, beyond the reach of mall cops. I felt a bit voyeuristic, as though I were looking through a hole in a bathroom wall.

This street was too busy for me to stay on it for long before I got discovered (not the starlet kind of discovery either, but the kind that ended badly), so I pulled my bag back on and trudged down to the end of the next corner. A few blocks away from the bars and restaurants would be quieter and I hoped to find a spot to settle in for the night.

I walked out of the commercial area into a residential neighbourhood. There were new brick condos, and then, along

a darker street, old run-down houses with rickety stoops. One
of them had a bunch of kids' toys on the small square of front
yard. Next to a lopsided snowman with sticks for arms and stiff
mittens hanging off the ends, sat a little yellow sled and a pail
and shovel, mini mounds of snow forming on them. I liked the
look of this house.

A narrow driveway separated the house from its neighbour,
and at the end was a free-standing shed-like garage. I went
around to the back of it and tried the knob on the door. It
turned. Just like that, I had found a place to sleep.

I stood for a minute inside the garage while my eyesight
adjusted. A little window allowed a shred of light from a
streetlamp to shine on a compact car, some shelves filled with
disorganized family junk and a bundle of drop cloths that I
could rearrange and use to soften the floor under my butt. The
garage was built directly onto the hard ground, but I put down
the cloths and some foam seat cushions I found and it wasn't
nearly as bad as sitting on the cement sidewalk. And, out of
the wind, a lot warmer than I'd expected. I was too exhausted
to worry about getting caught and I barely had to rationalize
my break and enter. I wouldn't take or break anything; I made
that vow to myself. I pulled my hands and arms into the body
of my jacket and huddled my back against the wall of the shed.

The thunder rumble of a garage door, and the sudden light
that burst through it, almost stopped my heart. I leapt onto all
fours, pulled on my pack, and jumped through the back door. A
concrete slab set into the ground led a few feet to an opening in
a cedar hedge. I slipped through and found myself sandwiched
between two rows of hedge. It looked like each neighbour had

decided to grow his own, and now both hedges ran the length of each backyard with a thin tunnel between them.

Hidden between the branches, my back pressed to the pack, against the hedge, I listened to a man whistling a tune. If he had seen me, he probably wouldn't be whistling, so I relaxed, letting my body sag.

I heard the car start with a reluctant grumble, and then the car door opened and closed again. He was going to let the engine warm up. I had to decide whether to start moving now, or wait until he pulled out and drove away.

I wondered what time it was and looked up through bare and lifeless tree branches at the sky decorated with pink and orange ribbons of cold light. I shivered and waited. I was freezing and tired, even though I must have slept soundly all night. I didn't remember waking up, and I didn't recall any dreams.

After I heard the car roll away, I started down the tunnel between the hedges toward the road. I couldn't believe my luck. I could get in and out of that garage without leaving a single telltale footprint in the snow.

I had to pee but it was too cold to think of squatting outside in a patch of snow. With my empty stomach knocking at me, I decided to go the few blocks to the restaurant where I'd eaten breakfast the day before.

First, I used the toilet at the back. Crouching in front of a low sink that must have been installed for a toddler, I washed my face and brushed my teeth with tap water. I had brought my brush but forgotten the toothpaste. The bristles felt good against my fuzzy teeth, but my mouth was still pasty and foul with morning breath.

In the booth at the back, the same waitress came to take my order. I pointed again to Number 5 on the menu, two scrambled eggs and toast, and she nodded and scratched the number on a pad. She was squat and had long grey hair pulled into a ponytail with a brown elastic. She looked bored and didn't ask me any questions. She stuffed the pad into her apron pocket, took the menu and walked away. I warmed my hands on another cup of scorched coffee. I imagined being a real person, with places to go, a daily routine and a voice. I would push my menu aside, smile, and say, "I'll have the usual."

I got the note I wrote the night before out of my pack, flattened it onto the tabletop and reread it. It still sounded okay.

The eggs tasted flat and I found I wasn't as hungry as I had thought, but I made myself chew and swallow, not able to bear the idea of paying for food I didn't eat.

I had survived my first night on the street. It didn't feel like a badge of honour, exactly, but it was something. Unfortunately, I'd also got myself a cough. Maybe I had caught a disease from that snotty kid's food-court hamburger.

The day before, I'd taken a transit route map from a kiosk in the mall. I spread it open at my elbow and traced lines with my fingers until I figured out the route number I needed to take and where to find the right bus stop.

I stepped onto the street from the restaurant and found the sidewalks clogged with people on their way to work, clutching briefcases like extensions of their right arms, and cups of Tim Horton's coffee: the elixir of life — or at least of punctuality. Everyone rushing to get to the job that paid for mortgages, vacations and big-screen televisions.

I had to flatten myself against the glass of a store window to let a man rush past. He almost plowed me right over, looking somewhere beyond me, as if I were invisible. I turned and peered into the glass. There it was, my face, floating, framed by the city street, a sewer smoking in the cold next to my ear.

My eyes looked shifty and dark in the orange-tinged reflection, a street-kid's face. A stranger.

I heard the whir of a city bus as it gained speed from one green light to the next. I turned and watched it rattle past me, crammed with people sitting and standing.

Too crowded. Dozens of people waited in glass shelters at the stops. I didn't want to get on a bus with so many people. I went back to the mall to keep warm and waited until the offices were full and bus stops empty.

⊸⊸⊸

The air brakes of the bus hissed and its body spat me out about a block from the police station. Even though my muscles were sore from so much walking the day before, my crotch felt better, less like raw hamburger. But my stomach was queasy and my head ached.

I had been to this police station before. After that terrible night. In one of its small blank rooms, Officer Davies had taken the piece of paper on which I'd tried to write the details of Granny's end.

Standing in front of the squat Lego-like building, I remembered the first time I'd walked up the grey stone steps and through the glass doors. Now, my shaking hands found my pants pockets and stuffed themselves inside, pressed against my hipbones. My raw nerves jangled.

If anyone recognized me as the girl who ran from the foster home, it would be game over. I'd end up at another crummy foster home, a halfway house or, worst yet, in jail on suspicion of setting that damn fire. I had to keep the hood of my sweater over my head and be quick. Like when I'd dumped Francine in the emergency room, I had to dump this note and run. Inconspicuously, of course.

I wondered if Officer Davies was in there, and if she'd remember me. She probably saw all kinds of people every day. Maybe even hundreds of victims and criminals.

My mouth had gone dry and I swallowed, hoping I wouldn't puke right in the foyer of the building. That would sure draw attention.

I made it to the top of the steps. A guy in a suit and long camel coat pushed through the door on his way out. He saw me and held it open, smiling, until I had no choice but to go through. I wasn't invisible after all.

The note was crumpled in my hand. I pulled it out of my pocket, soggy with palm sweat, and opened it, stretching the wrinkles out. The ink hadn't run, thank God.

I slouched up to the front desk. An officer behind the glass was sorting through forms, his back to me. I shoved the paper under the half-moon opening where glass met desk, turned and walked out. That was it. I'd done it.

I scooted around to the back of the building and caught my breath, waited for my heart to quit trying to beat its escape from my chest.

Low steel-wool clouds made the winter air warmer. I didn't want to waste more money on a bus, so I began to walk. I felt lighter; walking had become more effortless.

No one waited for me. I had no schedule, no school or work to go to. I had time. So much time I felt choked by it.

Already, I loathed the mall.

I had zigzagged and taken my time, looking in windows and going down side streets, to kill an hour walking the few kilometres back from the cop shop. Now that I was there — back among all the stupid stores and drone-people who shopped in them, the stink of frying food, the noise of mothers yelling at kids — I wanted to be somewhere else. But I wasn't ready to leave the city core, and the mall was about the only place that would harbour someone like me. I tried spending time in the big-box bookstore on the corner, but the staff followed me nonstop, jumping forward every time I touched a book, asking if I needed help.

Back in the mall, I watched the food court and I managed to snag another free meal before sunset. I was beginning to figure out the mall layout and exited the correct door this time, heading the same way as the night before.

It was probably a foolish waste of time to go to the same corner at the same hour. Char was no more likely to be there than she was the first time. But I wanted to try.

As I got closer to the spot, I saw some figures at loose ends standing in the cold. Not many people chose to stand around on Ottawa streets in late February, so I figured it must be the hookers. I slipped into the same doorway and took out my notebook and pen. On a piece of paper, I wrote her name with a question mark after it, hoping she hadn't changed her identity for the streets. For all I knew, she could be Angel or Cherry or Bambi.

Two women leaned against the limestone wall of an expensive dessert shop that was closed for the night. The first woman was black and skinny. She wore a puffy pink jacket that barely went to her waist and bubblegum stiletto heels.

The second one was overweight, her sausage legs stuffed into a pair of white go-go boots, her pale flesh melting over the tops like mushroom caps. The two of them must have been freezing.

"What you want, little girl?" the fat one asked. "Maybe you like to party, huh?"

I shook my head.

"If you ain't buying," said skinny, "you gotta clear out. You be bad for business."

I held up the piece of paper with Char's name on it, pushed it toward them. They crowded together and moved closer to read it. I wished then I had a photo of her.

"You lookin' for a whore named Char? We ain't seen no Char."

Across my knee, I flattened the paper, crossed out the short name and wrote her full name underneath. I held it up again.

"Charlene? Shit, that ain't different than Char, and we don't know no Char."

"Wait a minute, Wanda, I might. What about that Charmaine used to hang out around here? She real skinny?" the big girl asked me. "Long blond hair?"

I nodded and held my breath.

"She gone," said the black one. "She went off to Toronto with Manuel."

She must have noticed my disappointment because she said kindly, "Sorry kid."

The white one stepped toward me and said, "You looking for a place to stay, you pretty young thing? I know someone who can help you."

Knowing what she meant, I backed up, shaking my head and thinking about Morrow and Cooper and all the violations I'd had to endure. I'd die of hypothermia before I'd do anything like that.

I balled up the sheet of paper and tossed it in a trashcan.

As I left them behind, the skinny hooker said to her friend, "Let her go."

−⋅−⋅−

I wanted to sleep in the safety of the Morrison's garage again. I called the family Morrison because of a book I once read. My memory couldn't grasp the title, but I remembered the family name. There were a bunch of children and they all lived together. The parents were nice to the kids, and the kids had adventures together — in a tree house the dad had built, and around their neighbourhood. They put on plays in their backyard, solved local mysteries, that sort of thing. Granny had old Bobbsey Twins books around the house and I'd read them. This was a kind of a modern Bobbsey Twins family, but I didn't like the name Bobbsey. It sounded stupid.

The house lights were turned on and I imagined my Morrison family sitting around a big dining table, playing a board game and talking about their day. I liked the feeling of being close to such a family. Safe.

My body ached all over and my headache was worse. I bundled into the corner of the now-familiar garage, arranged the drop cloths under me and across my legs like a blanket.

When I finished tucking myself in, shifting and shoving to ball the fabric into the spaces to keep out the cold, I looked up. Tully, like a piece of magic, was leaning against the rusty fender of the Morrison's car.

"You okay?" he asked, his voice high and as beautiful as a song. He wore his bright red baseball cap — on backwards, as usual — and his favourite Hawaiian shirt. It was a child's short-sleeved shirt, but the sleeves still went past his elbows. His child's jeans were wrinkled like an elephant's trunk and puddled at the top of his white running shoes. He wore no coat.

"I'm okay." I heard my voice, this lie, as clearly as if I'd actually spoken it aloud.

"You have a beautiful voice, Annabel. I always wanted to hear it." Tully had never called me Annabel. My name, as it rode the wave of his voice, sounded foreign. As if he addressed someone else. "Can I come and sit beside you?"

"Yes."

I shuffled to make room and felt his warmth settle against me.

"What happened at the farm after I left?" I asked.

"I'm all right. The details don't matter."

"What's going to happen next?"

"No one can know," he said. "For now, I'll spend as much time as I can with you."

"I wish things had been different, that I'd known how important you were to me."

"I do too. I'm as guilty as you. I wanted to tell you a hundred times, but couldn't find the courage."

"Tell me what?"

I felt Tully squirm next to me like a schoolboy in sex education class.

"Living in a small body can make you scared of big things." He paused. "I love you."

I rested my forehead on my knees and sobbed. I could feel Tully's arm around my shoulder. I really could.

Chapter 19

They came through the black. Flashing red and white lights reflected in the snow on the ground and on the sides of innocent buildings. An assault of police cars. I imagined that could be the official term, like they were living animals: a herd of cows, a pack of wolves, a murder of crows, an assault of police cars.

I had stationed myself in an alley down the street from Cooper's apartment after twilight, about an hour before the cop sirens finally whirled through the night air. I had begun to think the police wouldn't come after all, that my note was for nothing and I'd get frostbite instead of resolution.

For the third night in a row it was crazy cold outside. Too cold to snow, and the wind whipped through every layer I wore, chilling me to the core. While I waited, I had to stifle coughing fits with my cupped palms so no one would hear me. It was risky to stand there at all, but I had to see it come to an end. For myself.

Earlier, I had watched as people went in, Fizzy and a guy named Dante, who always wore head-to-toe black leather. Fizzy didn't have a hat on and his electric hair sprang up and down in the cold as he walked. I felt sorry about Fizzy. He had been a little kind to me. He was generous with a smile or a wink, even if he could be condescending.

The police had stormed in and the blue door hung wide open. Jaundiced light shot a dim streak across the sidewalk. The first person who finally emerged was Cooper, handcuffed and angry, trying for dignity by wrenching his arm out of the officer's grip every time the cop grabbed hold of him.

Fizzy came out of the apartment, and Dante, Fizzy chatting with the cops like he knew them. Maybe he did.

And then came Graydon, small and pallid. Viewed from a distance, he looked like a scared child. I was sure he'd always looked so young and helpless, but I had chosen to see him as my white knight. When it came to him, I was as blind as I was dumb.

I told myself I was rescuing Graydon, not condemning him, and hoped it was true. He was as much a victim of his life as I had been a victim of mine. I wanted the pain to be over for us all.

The drugs Cooper bought, bagged and sold every Friday and Saturday night were nickel-and-dime shit. I knew that. Getting him arrested didn't undo the ache around my ovaries and the rip in my soul. Nothing ever could. But I'd done some damage, had put Cooper on cop radar, and that was something.

From the start I had known the painting business was three-quarters a sham. They must have painted sometimes because they came home covered in splotches. But not every time.

I coughed freely now. A rumble that sent plumes of breathy mist into the air around my toque.

A cop spread his hand over Graydon's head when he stepped through the back door of the police car, so he wouldn't bump it. That seemed kind but did Graydon deserve that kindness after what he'd done to me? The cop should have let him bash his head against the car.

"Let's go," Tully said, his hand in mine. "It's over."

❧❧❧

Tully came and went in the following days. When he was with me, we talked about Jerome, Mary and Bobby. We talked about the horses and wondered if they were all right. The fever that simmered and ate at my brain, or whatever caused the fever, made me sentimental, and I cried when I thought of Jett and his black-coffee eyes, soft with affection for me. He probably thought I had abandoned him.

I began to feel less and less real with each day that passed. I still got thirsty and gobbled free water from the tap in the mall washroom, but I stopped feeling hungry. I couldn't remember when I last ate.

The mall kept me warm, outside cooled me off, the Morrisons' car shed kept me safe. I lived without goals or ambition, waiting to see what might happen. I truly didn't want to know what joy or horror lay around the next bend.

Late on a weekday morning I was walking back to the shed from the mall when I got overwhelmed by tiredness and had to take a break. The day was fuzzy with cloud, and warmish; the temperature probably hovered around zero.

I slumped onto the sidewalk to catch my strength, rested my back against the brick wall of a multi-level parking garage. I swung my backpack off and set it next to me on the ground, my arm still looped in the shoulder strap in case thieving street people got any ideas. I chose a spot under an overhang so my butt wouldn't get too wet from the dirty melting snow.

I rubbed my face in my hands. I pulled off my toque and tried to run fingers through my hair but they got caught in

202

the tangled nest of knots. I hadn't gone for a haircut in forever and it was getting long. I needed to wash properly and change my clothes. All the stuff in my pack was as filthy as the set of clothes I had on.

Now that I wasn't paying for food, I could spare some change for the Laundromat and decided to head there and wash all my stuff. I probably stank like a sewer.

When I looked up, I saw a pigeon. It was an ordinary city pigeon with purplish-grey feathers and scaly little feet, but her beauty struck me with the force of a slap. I could hear the small burbling sound she made in her throat. She looked sleek, strutting close, staring at me with a hopeful black eye, scavenging for breadcrumbs on the sidewalk like I was. Both of us belonged somewhere else. Some place where the air tasted clean and the ground was made from earth and grass instead of cement and asphalt.

I coughed into my hand and she looked slightly startled but didn't move away. She seemed confident in her closeness to me. I could have reached out and touched her, but didn't want her to fly away. Not unless she took me with her.

A lavender eyelid flashed over the tiny black bead of an eye. I smiled at the iridescent beauty of her perfect lady's neck, and wished Tully was there to share the moment. I decided to put the image of my pigeon away and tell him about her when I saw him.

When the bird realized I had nothing for her, she strutted to the edge of the sidewalk and, startled by a passing car, flew away with a rustling, flapping noise.

I wiped away a cold tear and slumped against the building once again.

The people in the Laundromat eyed me like I was a criminal or a crazy person.

A college student had his study books spread out at a long table that people used to fold their clothes. He looked at me from under his gelled hair and made a face of disgust. I envied him his books.

A mother with a bald baby on her hip stood at the dryers trying to put the clothes in with one hand. I wondered why the college kid wasn't helping. I would have offered to hold the baby, but I got the feeling she would refuse.

The mother had thighs like cannons and her hip was a shelf for her kid. The child looked like an old man, wise and innocent at the same time. The woman appeared pregnant again, or maybe she hadn't recovered her shape from the first time. For all I knew, she had been that shape before she got pregnant.

I couldn't wash the clothes I had on, unless I wanted to stand there naked, so I shoved in the outfits I wasn't wearing. It would be a treat to have clean underwear again, even though I would have to pull it onto my dirty body. Sponge bathing in the mall washroom wasn't quite good enough.

I got a package of washing soap out of the dispenser and pushed my clothes into one of the washers.

When everything was all whooshing away in the machine, I sat on one of the black plastic and metal chairs and rummaged in my bag for *Heart of Darkness*. It was getting ragged. The backpack I had taken from Cooper had filth ground into the fabric. Living on the street was murder on your stuff.

I wished I could go back to the used bookstore and see Lyle's friendly face. But I couldn't. The embarrassment of returning without the books he had so generously lent me kept me away. He had suggested *Surfacing* and I had watched the letters blacken and disappear in the tin wastebasket in that hellhole of an apartment.

The moist heat inside the Laundromat made me itchy and hot, and I longed to take off my toque, but I didn't want the world to see my ratty hair.

I opened my book and hid behind it until the washer got the streets out of my clothes.

Homeless was only a "p" away from hopeless. That little "p" had caught up with me and I was spending less time out and about, and more time crushed into the corner of the Morrisons' shed, either talking to Tully or sleeping.

I was amazed at how infrequently the family used their small outbuilding. The car went out every morning and returned every evening, but that was it. Even though the shed-slash-garage was crammed with stuff, they never went in to get any of it. Some of their junk was broken and I wondered why they bothered to keep it. I imagined that Mr. Morrison fancied himself handy and planned to fix all their broken stuff, but he was always either at work or with his family, and never had the time. Some of the things were seasonal, like the kids' bikes and tricycles, and a set of faded lawn chairs. It sure wasn't bike and lawn-chair weather.

Either way, I was glad I could feel safe there.

On the last Thursday in February, I stole. I hadn't stolen anything before, unless I counted Cooper's backpack and Graydon's sweatshirt, which I didn't.

I got paranoid about the money. I had only twenty dollars left and didn't know what I'd do when it ran out.

I wandered inside the mall drugstore to warm up and got entranced by the huge wall of makeup. So much of it: tubes and bottles, creams and polishes, lotions. I wouldn't have known what to do with most of it. I pulled out sample lipsticks and twisted the creamy colours to the surface of the tube, colours that ranged from palest pink to darkest burgundy. I dabbed some of them on my hand, in the webbed space between my thumb and forefinger. I tried to imagine it on my lips, how I would look.

I jumbled all the lipsticks back into their slots and turned. Facing me were vast shelves of pain medication. I had never realized how many different kinds there were. The pain in my head was constant and I could hardly stand it. One little white bottle of Ibuprofen on the drugstore shelf begged me to lift it. I went for the cheapest one, the no-name brand knock-off.

Before my fingers touched it I was struck by a panic that the pills inside might rattle so loudly everyone in the store would hear me. They would all see my shame, what I had been reduced to.

But it made no noise at all as it slid from the shelf to my pocket. I walked out. I don't know how I got away with it, given how thoroughly ragged I looked.

I went to the washroom and took two of the pills with water. An hour later I felt better, had more energy. But Tully was angry with me.

"How could you?" he asked when we were safely back in our shed.

"Desperate," I told him, not meeting his eyes.

"You're a thief now, you know that? A criminal. You had the money. You should have paid for it."

"I was afraid. Leave me alone."

"You want me to leave you alone? You sure about that?"

"No! Don't go. I don't know what I'd do out here without you. I'm sorry I stole the pain killers."

"I won't leave you. I wish you hadn't stolen, but as long as you're sorry about it, I forgive you."

❧❧❧

I wandered and life whizzed around me. Cars drove off to important places, people hustled along. Only the homeless, destitute, lonely and aged were left behind. It was as if the entire world was in fast-forward except for us.

At the place on the Market where several streets came together in a confused traffic tangle, I watched an old man walk to the corner, dragging an oxygen tank on a wheeled cart. Clear tubes snaked into the nostrils of his craggy face. He shuffled to the curb, looked both ways, and set out across. A car that had been nowhere a moment before suddenly squealed its brakes and stopped, the shiny chrome bumper inches from his bowed knees. The driver, a man wearing a charcoal suit jacket and red tie, honked at the old man, actually raised his fist to him. The geezer held his head a little higher and made it to the opposite curb without a glance in the impatient man's direction. I almost applauded when the last wheel of his oxygen tank cart clanked its way to safety.

I walked to the next corner and spotted Willie. He had no legs and was in a wheelchair, but he had a dog. I envied him the companionship of his little mottled mutt with one blue eye and one brown. A sign on Willie's lap next to his tin can read, "My name is Willie. Please help." Sometimes he took out a battered wooden recorder and played a warbling tuneless noise. Maybe he figured people would pay him to stop.

Whenever Willie finished begging for the day, the dog jumped into his lap. Willie grabbed the dog's fur in his fists

207

and pulled him to his chest, and then let him go and told him gruffly to get the hell down. The dog dropped to the ground and danced in dizzy circles around the wheelchair.

Willie lived at the Men's Mission. I know because I followed him once. Generally, I tried not to go near the mission. Most of the men were as harmless as Willie, but some of the younger ones, the newly homeless because of drugs and alcohol, scared the daylights out of me. Especially when they were drunk or high, which was a lot of the time.

I watched all of this seething life, but nothing had anything to do with me. I was the ghost of someone forgotten. Abandoned and irrelevant.

After I started taking the pain pills, I felt a bit hungry and picked up a discarded morsel here and there from the mall food court. I wouldn't pay for food anymore. There was no way my old breakfast restaurant would even let me in the door now, although I didn't try.

⊷⊶⊷

I didn't know what day it was or what month. Weeks had passed since I'd left Graydon. It might have slipped into March without me noticing. The weather was up and down, as usual: one day snowy, the next icy, the next warm as spring.

One thing I always noticed was the condition of the street. In icy weather, the sidewalks were slick and treacherous; when it warmed up, they were slushy, and passing cars sent rivers of brown muck washing onto the curb, over the tops of my boots and into my socks. You couldn't escape the weather; it was as inevitable as death.

I woke up before dawn, my head and throat screaming. Slipping out of the shed before Mr. Morrison came for his car was essential, and I had got good at it. My internal clock nudged me awake in time to collect my stuff and skedaddle before Mr. Morrison clanked the garage door open. I rattled two pills out of my pilfered bottle and choked them down without water. The chalky residue scraped an unpleasant trail down my throat.

Getting to my feet made me shaky and dizzy. I settled my backpack over my shoulders and had to grab the doorframe to steady myself before I stepped through it. I felt old.

The snow between the Morrisons' hedges had gone soft overnight while the temperature rose. My boot sank inches into a receding patch of brown snow. My breath hung in the damp air, looking like a mini rain cloud, instead of getting instantly cooled by icy wind and disappearing.

My feet took me through the hedge corridor to the back of the property and I turned left in the laneway toward the street. Sometimes I turned right. I tried to vary my route, in case anyone inside saw me and got suspicious about the crazy-looking girl who had a habit of skulking around their house.

At that time of the morning, as houses and apartments emptied and schools and offices filled up, the streets were dangerous with traffic. I didn't like rush-hour busyness, but I had to be out of the shed until Mr. Morrison had come and gone. And, desperately thirsty, I needed a drink.

As I made my slow way through the crowd, I saw a red hat bobbing around at waist height a block ahead. Tully's face turned to me in a quick snapshot and then he was swallowed by bodies. I stopped and searched for him but he was gone. I kept walking and looking, and I saw him again across the street. His hat caught my eye, his small white face unmistakable in the mass of people. And again he was gone.

What was going on? He was too far away for me to see his expression. I didn't know if he was playing a game, or if there was a genuine emergency. Did he need me to follow him? Why didn't he come and tell me what was happening?

The pain in my head felt worse. Panic, and a little anger at Tully, rose in me. I pushed past people and jaywalked across the street to the place on the sidewalk where he had stood. There was nothing remarkable about the spot, no clues left behind.

I looked for him, agitated, standing on my toes and straining to see over the crowd. I spotted him again. Running. His legs and arms pumped like pistons as he ran to the corner. Without stopping, he ran straight into the road.

Drivers wouldn't see him. He was right in the middle of the traffic now. His red hat flashed in the crush of cars stopped for a red light. I had to rescue him. He'd never lived in the city. He didn't know how dangerous the road could be. No one would watch for him. No one cared.

I didn't have time to go to the corner or wait for the light to change so I dashed out into the traffic, making straight for the spot I'd last seen him.

I got there and he was gone again. Frustrated, I spun on the spot just in time to see the bumper of the car that hit me.

My legs seemed to disappear from under me, like a magician had conjured them away, and I went down in slow motion. I tried to keep upright but the scene in my vision tilted until there was only the steely sky.

The side of my head bounced off the asphalt and the clouds swam away.

Chapter 20

The room stank of disinfectant. And my legs were killing me because I was afraid to use the self-medicating morphine pump. Heroin helped to ruin Mama and I'd read that morphine was basically the same thing as heroin. Hopeless as I felt, I didn't need addiction too. But I nodded when the nurses asked if I was using the pump.

I thought I'd get used to the hospital smell and not notice it anymore. I had been there for three days and the stench still seemed as fresh as the moment I first opened my eyes.

I refused to eat because I didn't feel hungry, not because I wanted to be difficult. They gave me a pad of paper and a pen so I could communicate, but I had nothing to say to any of the unfamiliar faces that came and went. Whenever someone tried to speak to me or ask questions, I wrote *Mary Gervais* on the paper and held it up. When they brought a tray of food, I put up my Mary sign and pushed the food away.

They knew who I was. The little bracelet on my wrist had my name typed around it in light-blue ink: *Annabel Cross*. The name around my wrist felt like someone else's. But I reasoned that if they knew who I was, they had to know who Mary Gervais was.

My legs in their white casts stuck out like two Q-tips. A metal bar went from knee to knee, to keep my legs apart and together at the same time, so they would heal from their many breaks, or so said one of the doctors.

The only doctor whose name I could remember was the neurologist, Dr. Edwards. His eyes were soft and always looked straight into mine when he explained things. He had a voice like honey. The other doctors looked at my chart, the thermometer, a wristwatch, even out the window rather than meeting my gaze. I was too tired to listen to them anyway. Despite the pain, I was asleep for more hours in a day than I was awake, ever descending into the sleep of the exhausted, black and empty.

What would happen to me now; which foster home or halfway house would I be forced into? I wanted to go home. To Mary's. But I feared that bridge had been burned. Literally.

I was staring out the window at the tops of far-off trees when I heard someone come in. I turned my head and Dr. Edwards was at my elbow. He wore a crisp white lab coat, with a stethoscope tucked into a breast pocket, and a tie in brilliant jewel blue.

"Annabel, you probably won't remember this, but when you first arrived in the emergency room we took an MRI of your head. That's a kind of x-ray to make sure your brain didn't sustain any damage in the accident. At first, you presented us with a heck of a puzzle. Then we identified who you were and acquired your medical records. I believe we now understand what we saw on your MRI."

I waited with only mild interest. Did I have brain cancer or something?

"You might be pleased to know that we found the cause of your inability to speak. You have some old damage to your brain that's causing what's called *expressive aphasia*. It's common in stroke patients with damage to the area of the brain where your damage is. Some time ago, you might have suffered a stroke or other type of brain trauma which affected that area, probably coincident with the time of your grandmother's death."

He meant my grandmother's murder. I saw in his eyes that he was striving to be delicate. I thought of the day I got swarmed by those girls at the mall, how I threw up in the washroom and had a headache for days afterward. I thought of how I couldn't move when my mother's breath, full of stale fear, puffed onto my cheek and she placed the phone on my covers. Had I been paralyzed with fear, or was it something else? A stroke or the knock on the head? I supposed I might never know. But my brain had given this doctor the first clue. I hadn't been whole since that night, and I had known it.

"There's no cure but the good news is that you're young. We expect you'll respond to therapy and regain some speech over time. How much improvement you'll realize depends on a lot of factors."

Why had it taken two broken legs for someone to finally find out what was wrong with me? Anyway, I hadn't said a word in more than two years. In that time I had lost everyone I'd ever cared about. What did I care if I ever spoke again?

Stubbornly, I held my Mary sign in front of his nose.

"Yes. I've looked into that. Mary Gervais is not allowed to have contact with the children she was fostering. I'll keep trying. But you do need to eat, Annabel." He put his hand on my arm, the one that had my name on a bracelet around it.

I shrugged and looked at my IV bag, liquid antibiotic sliding into my veins, battling the pneumonia I'd got from a bout of 'flu. The streets were generous with their germs.

I wasn't hungry.

"If you don't eat, we'll have to put in a feeding tube. You don't want that, believe me."

When I half-agreed to eat, he left.

I wasn't consoled by his diagnosis, but at least people wouldn't assume I was faking this silence anymore.

⊷⊷⊷

During all my hopeless days without a home, not an hour went by that I didn't think about Mary or Tully, and wish one of them would rescue me. While I sat in my hospital bed, I didn't feel rescued; I felt kidnapped, or arrested and held against my will.

As promised, I began to eat. I could barely choke down the red Jell-O and the slice of white bread with butter. I wouldn't touch the watery soup that had globs of yellow fat floating on its tepid surface. And all the versions of meat that the kitchen came up with looked like some kind of science experiment gone horribly wrong.

I was slurping my lunchtime Jell-O out of its clear plastic container when the woman walked in. I recognized her immediately and dropped the Jell-O container and spoon onto the tray with a clatter. My heart seemed to speed up and my fingers trembled. It was the social worker I had seen in Mary's kitchen just before I ran away with Graydon. This time, a navy suit instead of a brown one covered her doughy flesh.

"Hello Annabel."

She held out her hand to me but I didn't take it. I let it hang awkward in the air between us, until she curled up her fingers and took the hand back.

"Yes, well, my name's Ms. Blackwood. Do you know who I am?"

I nodded and wrote *social worker* on my pad as if the very words were poison.

"Oh no." She laughed like she was nervous. "I'm the lawyer for your grandfather's estate."

My grandfather? There was someone I hadn't wasted much thought on in a while.

What estate? The world seemed to shift and tilt a little.

"Your grandfather held a considerable fortune when he died. He left it to your grandmother, but she, for her own reasons, didn't want the money. She put it into a trust fund for you. When you turn eighteen, you become the beneficiary of the entirety of your grandfather's estate."

I sensed my own astonishment in my gaping mouth and wide eyes. She invited herself to sit on the edge of my hospital bed. The mattress bowed downward with her weight.

"I can see you're a little overwhelmed at this news." She smiled. "I'll go over the details, the actual numbers, with you another time. Suffice it to say, since your grandmother's death and until your eighteenth birthday, you have been receiving, and will continue to receive, a monthly allowance. Mary was getting your allowance cheques until you disappeared. She used some of the money for your clothes, shoes and school supplies, and re-deposited the rest into an account for you. Since then, I've been managing things. The allowance will be more than enough for you to live on, on your own, if you wish. The court will consider you economically self-sufficient, which means we can apply for emancipation." She took a moment to look like a proud predatory bird, a fat one. "In other words, you might not have to return to foster care if you don't want to."

I didn't trust her; hell, I didn't know her. I had discovered that I couldn't even trust the people I knew well, let alone a stranger. I had put my life, love and happiness in the care of Graydon and he had turned out not to have my best interests at heart, to say the least. This woman's words had no meaning to me. For all I knew, I'd never see Ms. Blackwood again.

At the mention of foster care, I scribbled a hasty question mark next to Mary's name on my pad.

The lawyer's eyes went shifty. "Ah. Mary. Well, she ran into a spot of trouble regarding the fire on her property. They tell me that you're desperate to see her, though. I'll see what I can do. In the meantime, rest and get well."

She stood and pressed her hand onto my shoulder. I felt the heat of her palm through the thin fabric of my puke-green hospital gown. Despite the gesture, Ms. Blackwood didn't feel like a friend to me. She had been a demon in my mind for too long.

◦◦◦

Granny and Mama made it clear they'd hated my grandfather, though I'd never met him. He must have been a bad guy to have produced such a rebellious, messed-up daughter, and bitter and resentful wife. I'd had to live with all his screw-ups, so I figured I deserved his money. Granny's final kindness was in seeing that I got it and Mama didn't. I was pretty sure Mama had given up hope that the money even existed, so I didn't expect her to come looking for it. Looking for me.

These days, Mama was at the bottom of the list of people I wanted in my life. Below the mean nurse with the mole on her chin who woke me up to take my temperature at three in the morning.

"You're healing quickly," said a day nurse with an ID tag that had *Carmen* printed on it. "You'll be home before you know it." Home. Optimistic Carmen either didn't know or had forgotten my situation. She smiled at me while she waited for the thermometer to beep. This temperature-taking business was weirdly obsessive.

Carmen's smock-like shirt had cartoon teddy bears on it, like the pattern on a toddler's bib, and her hair was pulled into a hasty bun. Wiry grey hairs stuck out around her ears.

"Normal." She threw the disposable plastic sleeve of the thermometer into a trash box with a hazardous waste symbol on it, and put the device away. From a trolley of medication she took a Dixie cup with three pills in it — a red round one, a blue oval one and a tiny yellow one — and put it on my tray with a glass of water.

The morphine pump was finally gone, so I had relaxed a little. They gave me oral medication to manage the pain of healing, but I didn't really need it.

My legs had stopped hurting so much, but they itched something terrible. Yesterday Nurse Carmen had brought me a long knitting needle. After I took the pills, she handed it to me and I pushed the needle down into my cast and used it to scratch almost to my ankles. *Ahh.*

Carmen smiled and then her skinny butt sauntered out my door.

After I started to sleep a bit less, the hospital got horrendously boring. I wrote down book titles I could remember wanting to read, and Dr. Edwards himself turned up with five novels and two magazines for me. I lost myself in them as much as I could.

⊷⊷⊷

A therapist showed up one day, to help me work on finding my voice. Her name was Mandy and she looked my age, but had to be older. She was super perky, which I generally hated, but her chubby face and jolly nature coaxed sounds out of me that I wasn't even embarrassed about.

Her recurrent saying: "You get out of therapy what you put into it," almost made sense.

She worked with me every day. It was pretty intense but she encouraged me and finally I said a word. Hi. I said hi. Mandy clapped her hands in a solitary standing ovation and hopped around the room.

"Oh, Annabel, did you hear that? You said it, you really did! Well done."

I teared up at her genuine joy. Maybe there was hope for me after all.

By the end of my second week with Mandy, if I truly concentrated, I could say: hi, yes and no. I couldn't hide my smile every time a word came out. I'd never join Toastmasters, but I might manage an actual conversation with someone who didn't exist only in my mind.

Since I'd woken up in the hospital, Tully hadn't returned. I'd known he was an image in my head, a figment. But I missed him. As always, I wondered where he was in this physical world and whether he was happy. I ached all over with loneliness, for Mary, Tully and for Jett. My Jett who loved me unconditionally or at least for the price of half a carrot.

I didn't understand why Mary wasn't allowed to come and visit me. But I found myself excited at the prospect of Ms. Blackwood's next visit. I had been thinking a lot about the money and how I could buy myself some happiness. What I needed to know was where it ended. What was the limit; how much happiness could I afford?

The lawyer walked in while I was fantasizing about the horse farm I would purchase. I planned to take Jett with me, and build him a small stable near the house. I had even sketched the layout of my fantasy farm, like a little kid, because I couldn't help it.

"I have some papers for you to look over, Annabel." Ms. Blackwood was more casually dressed and looked better for it, a white blouse with a string of pearls at her throat, a pair of black pants. The outfit produced fewer bulges.

"Hi!" I said, pleased at the astonished look on her face. Her sudden smile at my accomplishment looked so authentic I allowed myself to like her a little.

When I began to look at the papers, I felt breathless and convinced that disappointment lurked in there somewhere. It always did.

She went through it all with me: my allowance, the bulk of the inheritance that I'd get on my eighteenth birthday, the terms and conditions. It came out to a whole hell of a lot of money. More money than I'd dreamed of. I searched but couldn't find a disappointment in it.

When she finished, I sighed and lay back against my wad of pillows.

"Yes," I said.

For some reason, words for concepts, like yes, no or okay, came to mind more easily than the word for an object. I could say thank you but struggled to grasp the word for chair or mushroom. Mandy called it *anomia*.

"Here," said Ms. Blackwood, handing me a small piece of lined notepaper folded in half. "I'm not supposed to do this, so you have to keep it to yourself. This is unofficial. Open it after I leave."

⊸⊷⊸

I unfolded the paper. It read: *Mary Gervais is not allowed to initiate contact with you. You, however, are not prohibited from contacting her yourself, at Noble Spirit Farm.* Below this, Ms. Blackwood had written the address and telephone number. I recognized the address but the phone number had changed.

I folded the paper along the crease Ms. Blackwood had made and put it into the drawer beside the bed.

Chapter 21

Rehab sucked wind and hurt like hell. I used one of my new words a lot: "No." I folded my arms and retreated into the seat of the loaner wheelchair.

"Annabel, the harder you work, the faster you'll improve." Harold, my rehab coach, was huge and shaved bald. He reminded me of Cooper, in looks only, thank God. His skin was dark chocolate but his teeth weren't perfect; his two front teeth had a space you could drive a truck through. His canines stuck out too far. And he was kind.

I had lived without talking for almost three years. I was adaptable. I reckoned I could live without walking for at least that long.

Harold had dealt with reluctant patients too many times I guess, because he could be even more stubborn than me, and very persuasive. He put a hand on each of the arms of my chair and squatted in front of me, his eyes level with mine.

"Listen, you want to get outta here, right? My job is to help you get your independence back. Do what I say and you'll walk straight out those doors, on your own two feet, and never come back. I know you love me and everything, but I'm sure you don't want to stay here forever."

He was right; I didn't.

He stood up and clasped his hands behind his back, swaying on the balls of his feet, looking cagey.

"You know, you can't get a drivers' license when you turn sixteen if you can't walk."

He had me. I had more words now. Mandy was that good a speech therapist.

"Yeah, all right," I said.

Harold wheeled me to a set of parallel metal bars. He helped me up and held my waist until I had a grip with each hand, my body between the bars. I still had a walking cast from knee to toe on my left leg, but my right leg was free. Putting weight on either leg produced exquisite agony that Harold assured me didn't do them any harm. He had explained the issue of "hurt versus harm."

"Remember," he said, "don't be afraid of the pain. You have to play through it."

Easy for him to say, sadistic bastard.

I hobbled to the end of the bars like an old woman with a walker. By the end of it, I was out of breath, my hair sticking to the sweat on my forehead. I plopped back into the seat of the wheelchair and allowed Harold to arrange my feet on the footrests.

"Happy?" I asked the top of his shiny head.

"Ecstatic."

He wheeled me back to my room. The rehab centre didn't smell as bad as the hospital, and I was glad about that. The people here were every age and from every kind of life.

On the way to my room, I spotted Lara through the door to the communal lounge. She shot me a wink and a thumb's up. She had a right to be upbeat: she was going home with her parents the next day. She was a twenty-year-old college student going home after six weeks in rehab because of a fractured vertebra from a car accident. She had a bad case of verbal diarrhea and a talent for gossip. Somehow, she got the dirt on everyone in there and told me all about them. She loved that I didn't interrupt or interject because it let her talk and talk. I surprised myself when I realized I would miss her.

⟿⟾⟿

"There's Carl."

We were playing checkers in the lounge. Lara pointed to a grey-faced guy with a sunken chest and a blank expression who was watching TV with a quilt across his lap.

"He used to be a businessman. You know, three-piece suits and silk neckties. One night, after an extra scotch and soda he took a left turn on a red light and smashed into a minivan with a family inside. Killed them all and crushed his spinal cord. Now he can barely pull a pair of sweatpants over his Depends."

I wondered what would happen to him when he got out of rehab. Would he take to begging on the streets in a wheelchair like Willie? Was it an accident like Carl's that had put Willie Out There?

Lara pointed out Gena, two years older than me, who had put her head through the windshield of her new Dodge the first time she drove it. The impact had erased her personality, along with her ability to walk and feed herself.

I don't know where Lara dug up all that stuff. I wondered if she filled in the blanks with her own details. It sounded like it could all be true.

Car accidents, the great equalizer, could happen to anybody and most of the people staying at the rehab centre were recovering from getting hit by a car or getting their car hit by another car. Lives forever changed in an instant. A split decision made or not made could cause so much loss.

Some of the people had loved ones who got killed in the same accident they had survived. Late at night, I listened to their sobs of guilt and grief.

Nighttime ate people up inside. Fear and loneliness surfaced and gained crystal clarity when the lights went out and silent darkness fell. My own loneliness was like a second person in bed beside me; it was so familiar, and it produced a hurt that felt worse than the pain in my legs.

◦◦◦◦◦

I shed my casts like snakeskins. Each new cast was smaller than the last and then the final one dropped off. By that time, casts had been part of my body for so long I almost missed them, although it was a treat to be able to reach down and scratch the flaky skin of my calf with my own fingernails.

On a warm Monday morning, Ms. Blackwood at my side, I walked into a wood-paneled courtroom on my own two feet (and a set of crutches) to plead my case. The room was smaller than I'd expected and the only other people there were the judge and a few other ragtag souls waiting for their cases to come up. No jury, like you might expect if you watched lawyer shows on television.

Ms. Blackwood argued my economic self-sufficiency and maturity. I could now speak and walk independently, and I had more than enough money each month for rent and groceries. I agreed to work toward getting my high school diploma and she announced that my brand new social insurance number had arrived.

The decision came quickly. Ms. Blackwood was appointed to help me manage things at first, but all of a sudden I was emancipated, and had the court documents to prove it. The judge simply agreed to let me go. No more foster care for Annabel Cross.

Ms. Blackwood came to see me at the rehabilitation centre a few weeks before the end of my scheduled program. She walked into my room with *The Ottawa Citizen* newspaper under one flabby arm.

"Let's find you an apartment, shall we?"

We went through the classified ads together, using a fluorescent pink highlighter to circle the ones that looked promising. I didn't want to live downtown, and the outer suburbs would be difficult to get around in without a car. Luckily, there were lots of places in between. We checked the map for the location before we circled a listing. Ms. Blackwood made appointments to see five places all on one day.

She signed me out of the centre that Wednesday morning and we drove to the first apartment.

"Annabel," she said as she turned into the entrance of the first place on our list, "are you nervous?"

"Why?" I asked.

"Because you're biting your nails up to the knuckles."

I stuck my hands between my knees.

The first apartment was on the twelfth floor and the elevator whirred and rattled so loudly I thought it might drop us to our death at any second. I couldn't imagine taking that elevator every day, so I was glad to see that the apartment was no good. It stank like a mixture of cat piss and stale beer, for one thing. Plus the kitchen counter was cracked, some of the cupboard doors were missing, and the toilet seat had a chunk out of it. I wondered how that could have happened.

I pretended I couldn't talk at all during the interview with the landlord and when we got back into the car I said, "No way."

"Not exactly the Taj Mahal that one, was it?" said Ms. Blackwood. "I hope the next one's better."

The next one was only a fraction better and we both agreed it was a no too. I was getting tired, my left ankle ached and I had three more showings to get through.

The last one we saw held promise. The neighbourhood, in Nepean, was a good mix of corner stores and video rental outlets, a grocery store and an Ikea, all within walking distance. The low-rise building abutted a cemetery. At least those neighbours would keep quiet.

It was on the fifth floor and the apartment itself seemed to sigh when we opened the door on it. The rooms — a living room, kitchen, bedroom and bathroom — were all bare and clean. Nothing was broken or missing. A large window in the living room looked out over the trees of the cemetery. I could see the tombstones, white angels poking out of the earth. I sat carefully on the bare parquet floor and a lone dust bunny, missed in the cleaning, blew past like a desert tumbleweed.

The apartment felt as lonely as me and I thought we might get along.

"Yes," I said.

"Are you sure?" asked Ms. Blackwood, joining me on the floor in her long orange skirt, which she hiked up to sit lotus-style beside me. I nodded.

"Wonderful. I agree. I think it's perfect." She took my hand and I let her. We sat there for one glorious moment, as friends, in the apartment that would be mine.

◦◦◦

Harold had signed my final release form. I hugged him, his muscles cement-hard under my soft, pale arms.

"Good luck, Anna," he said. I liked the sound of "Anna."

Ms. Blackwood picked me up in her little blue Mazda.

"We have one stop to make and then I'll take you home."

Home sounded like someone else's idea, as if it were a foreign concept and didn't have anything to do with me. The memory of the little apartment had faded. I had seen it only once, weeks before, and couldn't recall the layout exactly. I'd begun to think it wasn't any good after all, that I'd made a mistake. I thought of its emptiness and wondered what I'd sit on or sleep in.

Ms. Blackwood pulled into a parking space in front of the big Ikea store.

"Let's pick out something for your new home. Anything you like. I'm buying."

"No —"

"I insist. Now come on."

We walked through aisles and aisles of furniture, lights, accessories, and I couldn't decide on anything. Ms. Blackwood stopped as we neared the end of the store.

"How about this?" She held up a glass vase with a hummingbird etched on the side. "It'll come in handy. Someone's bound to want to buy you flowers." She touched a curl of my hair, which had grown longer and almost touched my shoulders.

I shrugged and looked at the toes of my sneakers.

She bought me the vase. "Thank you," I said when we got back into the car.

"My pleasure. Now, let's get you home."

I wiped the sweat of my palms onto the thighs of my jeans and then sat on my hands to stop them from shaking.

Late spring had brought tulips stretching out of the ground in people's gardens in a parade of reds and yellows. Lazy bumblebees, newly awake, stumbled from flower to flower. I had watched them in the garden at the Centre and saw them now, drunkenly determined, as we waited at the last red light before reaching my new home.

When the car stopped out front, I was frozen solid and couldn't get out of the car. I couldn't even manage to open the door.

Ms. Blackwood came around to my side and pulled the car door open.

"Come on. I'll help you." She held out her hand, and I let her grip my right arm and help me out onto the curb. Even though I was physically able to do it myself, I welcomed her touch.

I bit my thumbnail with abandon on the elevator ride to the fifth floor. I didn't care about pristine fingernails. This moment was my beginning and I was terrified I'd mess things up all over again. I was glad Ms. Blackwood didn't try to stop me from biting my nails.

The apartment door opened on my new life like the door to a fantasy in *Charlie and the Chocolate Factory.*

"Surprise!"

I almost fell over. Harold and Mandy threw streamers in the air and Ms. Blackwood put a firm hand around my waist so I wouldn't end up back in the hallway.

"What do you think?" she asked.

From where I stood at the front door, I saw a beige couch, a TV and a small lightwood table with four chairs. I felt my mouth hang open and didn't have the power to close it.

"The furniture was delivered last week," said Ms. Blackwood. "I picked it out for you. If you don't like it, you can exchange it for something else. It's yours. Mandy and Harold came by yesterday to help get the place ready for you. There's a bed and dresser in the bedroom too."

Astonished and speechless, I sat on my new couch that smelled like a furniture store. I cried.

They pulled the chairs out from the table and sat in a semi-circle beside me, waiting for me to recover. Mandy handed me a Kleenex.

"Thank you," I said.

"You're welcome," said Mandy, and reached out to pat my knee, her face full of a smile.

Chapter 22

Gravel crackled under the tires. In the rearview mirror I saw small stones tumble away from the car in a wake of dust.

I was close enough now to recognize the landscape. The sign to Noble Spirit was almost obscured by a thick maple branch that had grown across it in the year since I'd been here. Could it have been only a year?

I didn't need the sign to know where to turn. From this point to the house, I knew every bend and pothole. Familiar trees smiled and waved at me as I passed by, and I gave in to the urge to wave back at them.

I hadn't called ahead, so she didn't know I was coming. I was afraid she would refuse to allow me to come if I warned her.

The day was aglow with the orange early fall sun. The reaped fields stretched like a lumpy brown blanket beyond the road to a horizon of trees.

Mandy's car — that I was not supposed to drive alone — rocked over a set of bumps as I turned right onto the long driveway. On my sixteenth birthday, I took the written portion of the graduated licensing test and was supposed to have a licensed driver in the car with me at all times. After a probationary period, I would take the driving portion of the test and then, if I passed, I'd have a regular license.

Usually Mandy came over after dinner and let me practice driving with her. We'd head out from my apartment and she'd prompt me to turn on my indicator when I forgot. She told me when to brake and when to accelerate. It was totally irritating, but I loved her for coming to help me. She didn't have to do it. It wasn't part of her job or anything. After I practiced, I'd drive us to the Dairy Queen. I always had a hot-fudge sundae with peanuts and Mandy had a Dilly Bar.

Mandy was twenty-three years old and lived in her parents' basement.

"They're old fashioned," she said. "They don't want me to move out until I get married. I have my own entrance and there's a kitchen and sitting room with a TV. I can pretty much come and go. I pay rent and everything." She went on and on as if trying to convince me that she was an adult, even though she lived with her mom and dad. I knew she was an adult. She was more mature than a jerk like Cooper would ever be. More mature than my mama ever was.

Mandy was helping me with my schoolwork too. In September, I started classes at a new high school, where no one knew me as the weird foster kid who couldn't talk.

I'd pleaded with her to let me borrow her car until she gave in. I had to visit the farm alone, and I didn't want to wait any longer. I didn't even care that I'd be in gobs of trouble if I got caught. It all felt right to me, coming out here now.

The farmhouse loomed closer and I could see the right side of the white porch. I scanned the field and caught sight of little Nacho, his nose to the ground, eating grass. His head shot up when he heard the car, his blond mane now so long it fell to his knees.

I hadn't seen Jett yet. He was probably at his favourite spot by the stream, at the bottom of the far field. I felt joy bubble through me at the thought of our first meeting, certain he'd remember me. I had bought a bag of carrots from a roadside stall and I intended to spoil those horses rotten. I imagined the velvety feel of Jett's nose, his warm breath through the hairs on my arms.

I knew Tully wouldn't be there. Ms. Blackwood told me some of what had happened. Tully and Char were taken from Mary after the fire and she was investigated and charged with negligence. I felt responsible, at least in part. It began with me and the broken windows, continued with Jerome's near death from peanuts, and ended with me and Graydon running into the night. They let Mary go but wouldn't let her foster more children.

All that aside, I couldn't help picturing Tully sitting on the grass by the paddock in his red ball cap with an open book across his lap.

The steamy scent of horses wafted through the open window and I sucked the air into my nostrils, never wanting to breathe it out. That smell felt more like home than even my little apartment, which I now loved.

I stopped the car in the driveway out front of the house, my hands trembling. It occurred to me I was about to put my foot on exactly the spot where I'd first seen Graydon Fox stepping out of Bobby's truck. Who was that silent and lonely girl sitting on the porch that summer day?

The porch itself looked exactly as I remembered it, with its set of mismatched chairs, the overturned crate that Mary used as a table.

I got out and thumped the car door closed. I hoped Mary might hear me so I wouldn't have to go to the door, but she was nowhere to be seen.

I limped up the porch steps. Although my legs had healed from their breaks, the right was now shorter than the left. I had a limp and still do, probably always will. A forever reminder.

It was cool in the shadow of the porch. Goose bumps raised the hairs on my arms and neck, yet I felt dampness under my armpits.

Through the screen door I saw part of the kitchen and the living room couch where I used to lie reading for hours. I heard the kitchen faucet blast on and off and felt nervous that Mary was so close.

Ignoring the jittery churning of my stomach, I rapped my fist against the wood of the doorframe. I didn't think I could stand the echoing chime of the doorbell.

And then I saw her. Mary walked toward me, her face squinting into the afternoon sunlight to see who could be standing unannounced at her front door.

"Yes?" she asked, before she knew me.

I smiled and put my hand up in a wave.

"God in heaven," she said, pushing her fists into her throat, "Ghost. Is that really you, child?"

I nodded, stepping back to let Mary open the door to me.

"I'm sorry. I'm sorry. I'm sorry," she said, her eyes melting.

No one had ever apologized to me. It seemed like Mary was entirely the wrong person to be the first to do so. As she hugged me, I noticed I'd grown taller than she was.

I stepped back from our hug to look at her. She had lost weight. She didn't look exactly thinner, more like emptier, like a balloon that had lost some of its air.

"Hi," I said.

She looked astonished and pleased.

"Oh. That voice sure is music." She flattened a palm against my cheek. "And you, grown up so."

She hustled me to a chair on the porch. She went into the house and brought out a tray with a pitcher of lemonade and two glasses, a blue plate with homemade ginger cookies. We sat on porch chairs and crunched the cookies.

"It was my fault," Mary said, finally. "I shoulda told you. I was wrong to keep all those secrets about you kids. You might not have run if you'd known."

"What?" I asked.

"That boy, that Graydon Fox. He'd had some trouble with fires. He'd started a mess of fires around his old foster home. Him and an older guy got charged. The older guy got a slap on the wrist, but they wanted to put Graydon in juvie before I said I'd take him. He set that fire in the barn that night. I knew it all along. I never thought it was you. That's why you ran, isn't it? You thought I'd blame you."

"Yes."

She put her hands together as if in prayer. "Oh Lord, there's that sweet voice again. That lighter I found in your jeans that day was Graydon's, wasn't it? How could I have been so stupid? I gave it back to you. I had no idea you'd fallen for that boy. I was a silly, blind woman."

Graydon had set me up. He had started that fire to convince me to go with him. Up to then, he had counted on Mary to keep his secret, and she had, but I'd been to blame as well, covering up for him. If Mary had known the lighter was his, things would have come out differently.

I thought of the ashes and scorch marks I'd found in the metal wastebasket at the apartment. That hadn't been just from Cooper burning my stuff. It was from Graydon letting off steam by setting fires in it whenever he felt stressed out. I pictured his pale, scared face and thought of the hidden scars, raised and marble smooth. And I forgave him right then and there. I hoped that someone, somewhere could help him.

"It's okay," I said, putting my hand on her freckled ham-hock forearm.

Her other hand covered her mouth.

"You know, we couldn't have kids, Bobby and me, and I didn't think I'd know what to do with a baby. We decided on teenagers. I thought I could save you all. Everyone deserves a chance in this life. That's what I reckoned."

"You did okay," I said. "Look. I'm happy."

Mary did look at me then. Tears struggled through her lashes and tumbled free down her cheeks. She looked away and out toward the gravel road.

"I don't foster any more. They pulled me out of the program. Poor Jerome going to the hospital and not coming home, that was the beginning of the end. I still miss the kids but the responsibility was terrible."

We sat silently for a while, contemplating terrible responsibility. I remembered the first day Graydon came up the driveway in Bobby's truck, all heat and dust. I remembered his scrawny legs and oversized suitcase.

"She called me from Vancouver once, your mother. Back in February, before I changed the phone number."

"Yes?" *Vancouver.* I couldn't say the word. I didn't know what to say. I wasn't prepared to hear this. Did I even want to know?

"She didn't sound good, Ghost. Not like when I talked to her the first time. In fact, she sounded really bad. With you and the other kids gone, it wasn't any use for her to call me about you. I gave her Ms. Blackwood's number."

I looked down at the porch boards between my feet, the paint still peeling, and felt Mary reach over and take my hand. We sat for a while longer, a sweet summer breeze rustling the bushes by the side of the porch rail.

Mary's gaze met mine once again and I remembered the other reason I had come to the farm.

"Jett," I said, holding up the bag of carrots I'd brought with me from the car. I looked over Mary's shoulder, past the porch lattice, and toward the paddock.

"Oh, honey, no. Jett's gone."

Gone? What did that mean, gone?

"He died in the spring."

I choked on a sudden trickle of lemony spit that touched the back of my throat.

"I'm sorry. Jett was old," she said. "His heart gave out one night and Bobby found him in the morning, curled up beside the stream, his nose near the water. You remember how much he loved that spot."

I remembered. It felt like my heart would give out too.

"Bobby put a cross under the willow tree to mark the spot, if you wanna go see."

I nodded and Mary let me go.

⇄⇄⇄

I touched the white cross. Bobby had done a nice job. The wooden marker was small, but sanded smooth and had bevelled edges. He'd given it a thick coat of paint that glowed white in the crystal afternoon sunlight. He hadn't put Jett's name on it. It was only the cross itself, white and lonely on Jett's favourite spot.

I sat on the flat rock beside the stream. My ankle throbbed so I pushed my left leg straight and nestled my heel into the soft earth. I didn't cry. I wanted to remember Jett's brown eye, clear as a marble when I pressed my ear against his shoulder and looked through it. Each eye was framed by long lashes, mascara thick and tawdry as a hooker's. He was so vain. I laughed out loud. Who would Nacho tease now?

I remembered the feel of Jett's nose against my lips, soft and fuzzy as a new kitten.

When I got up from the rock, I laid three carrots next to the cross, blew my boy a last kiss and limped back to the house.

He had been my boy. Part of me had survived so I could see him again. But I had arrived too late. Peace out, sweet Jett, and sleep tight.

Epilogue—2008

An earthworm wriggles blindly in my palm, struggling for freedom and the safety of black dirt. I place him gently on a mound of earth to the right of where I'm working. The next time I look, the worm has gone.

My wicker basket is almost full. I already harvested the day's crop of green beans, tomatoes and cucumbers. I weed as I go along. I bend to the last of the work and the carrot that I haul out emerges long and dirty orange. With it comes the scent of clean soil, loamy and natural.

I love my small vegetable garden, which supplements our meals during the summer months; I even can some things to eat during the winter. The raspberry bushes produce enough to make a dozen jars of jam easily.

I stand straight and hood my eyes with my hand against the glare of the sun, looking out toward the road. There's still no sign of him, but he won't be late. He never is. I glance at my watch. I have to hurry.

I pluck the vegetable basket from the grass and walk toward the house, glancing at the field as I go. Nico is stock still, his ears pricked forward and nostrils aflame. He was my first, a dapple-grey I got from a woman whose children had grown and moved away. She didn't have the time or inclination to look after him and, even though she loved him still, she let me take him.

I've rescued four darlings now: Nico, April, Falstaff and Glencoe. When I acquired these old, ruined and unrideable horses I realized that I would probably never learn to ride. I don't care. I have vowed to gather the abused and neglected to me, the way Mary did with her horses, and with us. I still have the Pony Club book she and Bobby gave me for my fifteenth birthday, and read it for the horse care information it contains: grooming, feeding, veterinary schedules.

In the kitchen, the vegetables tumble from my basket into the sink and I wash them and set them aside. I'll chop what I need after I get cleaned up.

I walk upstairs to my bedroom, with its view of the paddock and my horses. I strip off my clothes and drop them in the laundry basket.

Shower water streams over my skin, my breasts and thighs, smoothing away the scents of my garden and the horses, leaving behind lavender soap and honeysuckle shampoo. He loves the smell of my shampoo, but not more than the smell of the garden on my skin.

I towel off my hair, which I keep long, past my shoulders, and pull a tangerine cotton dress over my head. I choose it this afternoon because he likes it. He always says I look like a sunset when I wear it. I stripe eyeliner under my lids and peach lipstick on my lips.

I am no longer afraid of being a woman.

By the time I go back downstairs to the kitchen he's running water over his glasses and cleaning them with the hem of his untucked work shirt.

"Hurry," I say. "Everyone will arrive soon."

"Right. I'll take a quick shower." My husband walks toward me and I bend into his kiss.

Tully and I, grown to the age of freedom, have found each other once again. I wasn't able to rest until I tracked him down. I dug and dug, eventually finding his address with some help from Ms. Blackwood.

She was with me in the car when I pulled up outside his last foster family's suburban house. I sat nervously in the driver's seat, contemplating getting sick in the grass. But when I saw him come out unbidden onto the concrete steps — as if he magically knew I was waiting for him — I felt only relief.

I got out of the car and dropped to my knees, and we embraced on the front lawn.

"You're not a ghost," Tully said into my ear. "I won't let you be a ghost anymore."

It was time to take back my name. If I were safe, I could be Annabel once again. I shortened it to Anna.

I had barely dared to hope it, but Tully loved me. He did. And we had no one and nothing standing in our way. We were married in the garden at Noble Spirit Farm. Mary and Bobby, Harold and Mandy, Ms. Blackwood, and a few other friends we had made, sat in white plastic chairs and clapped after our first kiss. I smiled until I thought my face would crack. I couldn't help it. Tully cried.

My inheritance money bought us this small hobby farm and it supported him through teacher's college. Now he teaches English at the same high school where Bobby still has a class in wood shop. They are colleagues, and we laugh about that.

Mama died. Ms. Blackwood told me. A few years after Tully and I moved to this property, she got a call from a hospital in Vancouver that Mama had OD'd. Hospital staff had found Ms. Blackwood's number scrawled across the back of a photograph of a little girl, and a kind nurse decided to call. Mama kept a photo of me with her to her dying day. That was something.

The evening I found out, I lit a candle for Mama. Then I decided to pull out more candles. I lit one for Granny, Char and Jerome, and for Graydon and even for Cooper. Tully and I switched the lights off and sat in each other's arms in the warm glow of half-a-dozen candles. Without words, we remembered the people who had come and gone. I prayed for the living.

I'm chopping vegetables for the salad when I hear the shower water start. Earlier in the day I set the table, a big maple table with room enough for a large family. I gave the small apartment-sized table to Mandy, the one that Ms. Blackwood had bought for me. I had paid her back for all the furniture, I could afford to, but I didn't return any of it to the store. It had all been perfect.

Mary and Bobby will arrive for dinner first. They have the shortest distance to travel and Mary is punctual to a fault. I rinse out the vase with the hummingbird etching because Mary will give me a bouquet of flowers from her garden. She always does.

Mandy and her husband Paul will arrive next. They married a year and a half ago, and Mandy finally got to leave her parents' basement. They'll bring their baby and I'll hold her and bury my nose in her soft, powdery curls.

Maybe there will be a baby for us one day. Tully's apprehensive about it, afraid our baby will be born with dwarfism, like he was. I'm not afraid. I know I'll love a small baby as much, if not more, than an average-sized child.

Ms. Blackwood will arrive last because she's always late. For a lawyer, she isn't too hung up on getting places on time.

When I set the bowl of salad on the table, I hear Tully's footsteps on the stairs. We will greet our guests together, hand in hand.

Photo by Jeff Wissing

CAROLINE WISSING has a BA in English Literature from Queen's University as well as a diploma in Print Journalism. She became a technical editor and writer in Ottawa's intermittently thriving software industry, where she has worked for more than twelve years. Two of her stories, "Surrender" and "Gemini", received second and third place in Ottawa's Audrey Jessup short crime fiction contest. Wissing lives in Ottawa, Ontario.